Eva & Deray
A Different Kind Of Love

Tina J

Copyright 2019

Warning:

This book is strictly Urban Fiction and the story is **NOT**

REAL!

Characters will not behave the way you want them to; nor will

they react to situations the way you think they should. Some of

them may be drug addicts, kingpins, savages, thugs, rich, poor,

ho's, sluts, haters, bitter ex-girlfriends or boyfriends, people

from the past and the list can go on and on. That is what Urban

Fiction mostly consists of. If this isn't anything you foresee

yourself interested in, then do yourself a favor and don't read it

because it's only going to piss you off. ☺☺

Also, the book will not end the way you want so please be

advised that the outcome will be based solely on my own

thoughts and ideas. I hope you enjoy this book that y'all made

me write. Thanks so much to my readers, supporters, publisher

and fellow authors and authoress for the support. ☺☺

Author Tina J

More books from me:

The Thug I Chose 1, 2 & 3

A Thin Line Between Me and My Thug 1 & 2

I Got Luv For My Shawty 1 & 2

Kharis and Caleb: A Different Kind of Love 1 & 2

Loving You Is A Battle 1 & 2 & 3

Violet and The Connect 1 & 2 & 3

You Complete Me

Love Will Lead You Back

This Thing Called Love

Are We In This Together 1,2 &3

Shawty Down To Ride For a Boss 1, 2 &3

When A Boss Falls in Love 1, 2 & 3

Let Me Be The One 1 & 2

We Got That Forever Love

Aint No Savage Like The One I Got 1&2

A Queen and A Hustla 1, 2 & 3

Thirsty For A Bad Boy 1&2

Hassan and Serena: An Unforgettable Love 1&2

Caught Up Loving A Beast 1, 2 & 3

A Street King And His Shawty 1 & 2

I Fell For The Wrong Bad Boy 1&2

I Wanna Love You 1 & 2

Addicted to Loving a Boss 1, 2, & 3

I Need That Gangsta Love 1&2

Creepin With The Plug 1 & 2

All Eyes On The Crown 1,2&3

When She's Bad, I'm Badder: Jiao and Dreek, A Crazy

Love Story 1,2&3

Still Luvin A Beast 1&2

Her Man, His Savage 1 & 2

Marco & Rakia: Not Your Ordinary, Hood Kinda Love 1,2

& 3

Feenin For A Real One 1, 2 & 3

A Kingpin's Dynasty 1, 2 & 3

What Kinda Love Is This: Captivating A Boss 1, 2 & 3

Frankie & Lexi: Luvin A Young Beast 1, 2 & 3

A Dope Boys Seduction 1, 2 & 3

My Brother's Keeper 1. 2 & 3

C'Yani & Meek: A Dangerous Hood Love 1, 2 & 3

When A Savage Falls for A Good Girl 1, 2 & 3

Eva & Deray 1 & 2

Blame It On His Gangsta Luv 1 & 2

Eva

"Ok ma, that's enough." My sister Lenore said to my mother as she continued fixing her dress and veil for the wedding.

Lenore is one of my younger sisters, and the twin to Marcellus. My mom had three more kids after that and I'm happy she was finished because nine of us were enough.

Evidently, my parents would've had more children had some bitch not sent a demon after my father and had him killed in the human world. My mom told me the story about how she tried to keep him human for as long as possible but after the accident, she couldn't due to the extent amount of injuries. I still remember that day like it was yesterday. Witnessing my father dying was a scene I'd never want anyone to see.

Anyway, like the rest of us Lenore was matched up with a human by my grandfather Ambrogio. The two met in high school, which I'm shocked about because my parents didn't allow us to attend public school, but then again, we were off the chain in the beginning.

Especially, Caleb and I. We were beating the crap outta kids in public and vampire school. It didn't help when my cousin Niles and his siblings joined us. We were a forced to be reckoned with and no one bothered us. Lenore, Marcellus and the last three were brought up the same as us, but my parents were able to maintain their aggressiveness somehow.

The guy Lenore had to change was handsome and of Spanish descent. His family owned a few bodegas and he too had a few siblings. The night our families met, they were very nice and even asked if we heard about vampires living among us. I think deep down they may have known it's what we were but never said anything. Long story short, he fell head over heels with Lenore and it was before she had to mention him being changed.

Now that he's one of us, I swear he's more protective of her then before. He gotta know where she is at all times and they have six kids already. If he didn't have to be changed he wanted as much as possible; talking about Spanish people have a bunch of kids. All I could do was laugh because it does seem that way. If she really wanted more it's a way to do it but I think she was finished having kids.

His family also wanted to be vampires in which my grandfather had no issues in doing. He said the more the merrier because with the war coming, we'll need as many vampires as possible. Yup, the humans have tried for years to end us but we continue to grow state to state and even countries so there's no stopping us.

"Lenore you look beautiful." My mom started crying.

"Come on Kharis damn!" My father said and grabbed Lenore's hand. My mother was extra in every wedding.

"You ready Selene?" I asked my daughter who was sitting on my lap watching a kid show on the phone.

Oh yea, I had four of my own kids from a loser ass baby daddy named Faine. Yes, vampires have deadbeat daddies too. If I could kill his ass, I would. Unfortunately, my kids love him and my father said just because he can't commit doesn't mean he should die. I beg to differ.

The purpose of changing humans, is to have the guy fall in love and live happily ever after, not lie and cheat. It's crazy because he was the exact opposite once he changed.

Don't get me wrong, he was everything I wanted in a man when we first met. He reminded me of my father, by how caring and attentive he was. We went out on dates, he charmed his way into the family, etc.…

For some reason he became defective because once I turned him, he couldn't stop cheating and became this arrogant son of a bitch. Of course, I let his ass know what the fuck it really is and put him in his place.

Now he don't fuck with me and comes to see the kids when he feels like it. He's one of those men who says, *if he can't have me then he'll deal with the kids whenever*. I don't get it because he did have me and fucked up. I guess he thought I'd stay around but not me. And one thing I don't play about is my kids, so fuck him.

"You're next Eva." My mom said and kissed my cheek.

"She isn't getting married." My father winked his eye at me. The two of us always had a separate relationship then he did with the other kids. He and I were very close and I'm definitely daddy's girl regardless of how many kids they have.

"Don't say that Caleb. I don't want my daughter lonely."

"Maaaaaa." I hated when she said that.

"Eva isn't marrying none of these losers. She needs a man who's gonna boss up on her." Lenore said applying lip gloss.

"What?" I had my hands on my hips.

"Eva you're the only woman I know who wants to be the man in your relationship."

"That's not true." Everyone stared at me and I became offended.

"It's exactly why you and Faine didn't work."

"Faine and I didn't work because he's a loser and thought he was God's gift to women."

"You thought it at one time."

"Whatever." I waved Lenore off and she walked over to me.

"I'm serious sis. You're strong willed, overprotective, used to getting your own way, thanks to daddy." We looked at him and he shrugged his shoulders.

"And no man has been able to give you mind blowing sex that will have you looking for him with a flashlight."

"Lenore they're kids in here."

"Ma, they're not paying us any mind." She was right. They were playing by the window.

"It's not that sis. I just haven't found the right guy. I thought Faine was the one but…"

"But he couldn't make that body shake." She grabbed my father's hand and my mother busted out laughing.

"I can't stand y'all."

"We love you too Eva and we're gonna get you married. I love you sis." She blew me a kiss and all of us lined up.

"You ready?" My father kissed her forehead. I blew my breath and thought about what they said. Is it true? Am I waiting for someone to boss up on me? *Hell no!* That shit ain't gonna work because ain't no man about to boss me around.

****

12

"What up sis? You coming out with us tonight?" Caleb Jr. asked. We called him Cal because he got tired of answering my mom when she called my dad's name. He claimed he needed his own identity.

"Not if you and Niles are gonna be eating in public." I hated when they fed off people wherever we went.

"We don't do it all the time."

"Nigga anytime somebody piss y'all off in the club, what's the first thing you do?" He tried to ignore me.

"Exactly! Y'all take them outside, eat them, then do mind compulsion on everyone. I could stay home for all that."

"Nah tonight we're meeting up with this dude who just came into town. Supposedly, he opened up the new strip club Fangora and wants to have a sit down about this so-called war." My antennas went up.

"Fangora? Could he be any more obvious?"

"Hey, it's his club."

"How does he even know about the war?" I asked because my grandfather only told our inner circle about it. He

13

wanted everyone prepared but until he knew for sure the day it would happen, he didn't wanna worry anyone.

"Eva almost every vampire knows we're going to war."

"Yea, but that's in general. How does he know for sure what's coming?"

"I don't know, which is the exact reason you need to come." He scooted his chair closer.

"Eva, I maybe the oldest but you're stronger and smarter than everyone." I smiled because he's right. I'm not saying my family is dumb but I did tend to stay in the vampire library a lot growing up. I've learned about shit the elders weren't even aware of. I spent an excessive amount of time learning about fairies too. The powers a fairy possess are outta this world.

"Just come and if something's not right, then we can kill them all. You know we got the extra powers to do it." For those of you who haven't read Kharis and Caleb here's a breakdown of who we are.

My mother Kharis was sent by my grandfather Ambrogio to turn my dad, who is his best friends' son. In the process, my aunt Irina had to turn his best friend as well. Once my dad was changed, he found out his mother was a fairy, so now he or should I say, all of us except my mother are known as Faepyre. It's what people called kids when a Vampire and Fairy mix. We have both vampire and fairy powers and I must say the number of things we can do and see is amazing.

My father was human too when all of us were conceived, therefore we still have a lot of human tendencies. For instance, we still take showers, sleep from time to time and eat regular food. Granted, the food had to be bloody to get the full affect, otherwise; we'd only be able to taste half of it. We were also allowed outside day or night due to us being hybrids.

Our drugs and alcohol were different because what humans considered diseases, are what vampires used to be under the influence. The different type of cancers, diabetes and so forth are liquor and beer to us. Drugs are only used for us to use on humans unless it comes in liquid form because then it can be used to get us high. I know it seems like a lot but you'll need to know this reading our story.

"Cal he better be legit or I promise not to meet anyone else."

"You worry too much."

"You don't worry enough." Him and my cousin Niles never worried about anything. I wished I had the trait to live carefree.

"You coming cuz or what?" Niles took a seat on the other side of me.

"I guess. If I don't who's gonna watch the two of you?" I gave them a fake smile and they both told me to fuck off.

"Whatever you do, don't bring that crazy bitch Nicole." I put my hand against my chest like I was offended.

"Cal you know she loves you."

"She loved me so much she got pregnant by someone else." He spoke of my best friend. Well we aren't as close anymore after what she did to Cal. We did still hang out every now and then though.

"I'm telling you if she comes around, I'm gonna eat her ass up and not in the way she may want."

16

"Damn Cal. You still hurting off that shit?" Niles asked and we both looked at him.

"Y'all know she was supposed to be my wife."

"It's ok bro. We're gonna find you someone else. Maybe we'll get you a white girl like Niles."

"Yo! Don't come for my wife. And for the record, she's mixed with Italian."

"Nigga she still white." Cal said and we laughed.

"Italian."

"If her skin is white, then nigga she white."

"What the fuck ever."

"I ain't mad though because she can cook her ass off. Plus, her sister can suck a mean dick."

"CAL!" I shouted.

"She really can."

"Niles, I know damn well you didn't fuck your sister in law."

"I didn't but she did suck my dick one night."

"I can't believe you."

"What? They're identical twins and I thought the bitch was my wife." Cal and I shook our heads.

"I'll tell you my wife got her beat though. The things my wife can do is…"

"Ok Niles. I do not want to know anything Kat does in the bedroom with you."

"Anyway, be ready around ten." He stood and walked away.

"Cal you better not fuck your in laws when you get married."

"I'll try not to." He left me sitting at the table with my mouth hanging open. What type of men are they? For the rest of the reception we partied hard, and as bad as I didn't wanna go out, I dropped the kids off to my parents and went home to change. This guy better be worth the trouble.

Caleb Jr. (Cal)

"It's about time." I yelled at Eva when she came out the door. We could've flown to the club and got there in five seconds but we tried to act human as much as possible.

"I had to drop the kids off and get ready. Duh, we all left at the same time." She sat on the passenger's side and closed the door.

"Where's Niles?" He gave me a look.

"That's his fault for cheating on her." I laughed because anytime we went out now, Niles wife Kat had to come with us.

He cheated on her a few times and she vowed to leave him if it happened again. Of course, he wasn't about to let her walk out his life and stopped. However; Kat still didn't trust the women out here and whenever we stepped out, he either made her come or she invited herself. He didn't care though because he was too scared to lose her.

I think Eva and I are the only ones in the entire family not married or even in a relationship. Well, she was and kicked the nigga to the curb and me, well, the bitch cheated.

19

Nicole was perfect for me in every way possible. She was pretty, could sex me good, cook and wanted to spend her life with me from what she said. The only problem was she wanted kids and as a Faepyre, I couldn't give her that right away.

The women were able to reproduce right away with a human, where men had to get a certain potion made up to release the sperm. It's because even though we're part human, the sperm is frozen inside of us. *I know its crazy right?*

Anyway, Nicole didn't know I was different and I planned on keeping it that way until we were married. I did any and everything to make sure she never found out and my family never mentioned it either.

I told her we could have kids once we're married because I didn't want kids and not be together. It was the only excuse I could come up with.

Evidently, she wanted kids bad because she went out and fucked another human, got pregnant and brought her ass to me claiming the child to be mine.

"Cal how can you say the baby isn't yours?" She showed me the stick with the pink lines going across indicating she's expecting. I walked away and headed out the door.

"Nicole, I always pull out and I had condoms."

"Cal, I didn't sleep with anyone else so how am I pregnant?" I laughed and turned around.

"Nicole it's not my baby and you wanna know how I know it's not?"

"It is yours but I'll entertain your theory." She folded her arms across her chest.

"I can't have kids. That's how I know it's not mine."

"Since when you couldn't have kids?"

"Since forever. It's the reason I wanted to wait until we were married. I was gonna tell you and we could go from there." Instead of responding, tears raced down her face because she knew she was caught.

"I know you wanted kids in the future Nicole and I would've done anything you needed to make sure you had some, even if it meant adopting, but sleeping with another man isn't what I had in mind."

21

"Cal." She tried to speak and I put my hand up.

"Three years down the drain because you couldn't wait." I wiped the tears on her face.

"You were supposed to be my wife. We were gonna grow old together and raise a family in the country but you were in a rush." I kissed her forehead and opened the door.

"I'll get rid of it. Cal just don't leave me." She was holding onto my neck.

"I can't do it Nicole because all I'll see is you giving your body away to someone else."

"Caleb don't do this. Please. We can move past it." She started crying harder and it was tugging at my heart. I may have been able to move past it if I cheated on her too but I never did. My father always told me, when you love someone don't ever make them cry and cheating would've definitely made it happen.

"Who was he?" She shook her head no.

"Tell me Nicole." She still wouldn't tell me. I lifted her head and stared in her eyes.

22

*"Who did you fuck?" I was doing mind compulsion on
her and when she said his name, I dropped her to the ground
and drove to his house.*

*The minute Brian opened the door, I beat him like a
nigga off the street, then called a few newbie vampires over
and had them dispose of him. I can forgive a lot but my best
friend fucking my girl isn't something I could. The only reason
I didn't kill Nicole is because she was pregnant and my mother
would kill me for murdering a child.*

"CAL!" Eva shouted bringing me out my thoughts.

"Why you yelling?"

"Ugh because we're here and you haven't moved out
the car.

"Oh, I was thinking about something." I stepped out
and walked over to the car Niles and Kat were in.

"I'm telling you right now if one bitch even thinks
about trying me, I'm gonna fuck you up." Eva and I started
laughing. Niles hasn't cheated since she was gonna leave him
the last time but it didn't stop the women from talking shit to
Kat.

"A'ight damn Kat. You act like I tell them to fuck with you."

"You did in a way by fucking them. I swear if we weren't different, I would've killed you already." Niles waved her off and left her standing with Eva.

She was one of us and always said she couldn't kill him now because someone would always save him. If he were human, he'd die right away. We knew she was talking shit because if she wanted to leave, she could've.

My aunt Irina told her plenty of times she'd put a cloak on her so he couldn't find her but she never did it. My uncle told Niles, he better get it together because he went through the same thing with his mom and she left him and got revenge.

"What you do now?" Security removed the velvet rope for us and you could hear people whining and complaining about us getting right in. The perks of being popular pays off.

"I changed my phone number and she assumed it was because some bitches had my number." I gave him the side eye.

"Hell no! I ain't crazy."

"Then why you change it."

"Nigga, I wasn't happy with the Galaxy so I got me an Apple iPhone." He showed me the new phone and the shit is nice as hell.

"You could've kept the number."

"When have you ever known me to keep anything I changed?"

"True." He never kept anything that wasn't brand new.

For instance, he got new rims for his truck and instead of putting them on the truck he originally got them for, he went out and brought a new one. He ordered a new desk for the office in their house and once it came, this nigga changed the entire room around and added new furniture. His ass got OCD or something because he did it with everything.

"Anyway, when dude coming?"

"Why?"

"It's too many bitches in here and I don't need Kat thinking I wanna fuck any of them, even though I wouldn't mind."

"Wouldn't mind what?" Kat stood in front of him and he smiled.

"I wouldn't mind taking you in VIP and fucking the shit outta you."

"What you waiting for and are we having company?" She asked about one of the strippers.

"Stop playing Kat." They never had a threesome and he'd always get mad when she mentioned having one. She didn't want one but Niles always told her no other bitch or nigga will touch her so she loves saying it to piss him off.

"Kat ain't nobody got time to be breaking up you two fighting, cuz y'all in her thinking of ways to piss one another off." Eva put the drink to her lips after speaking.

"Fine!"

"Kat, I promise you're gonna make me fuck you up." She whispered something in his ear and the attitude went away quick.

"Damn nigga. All she gotta do is say one thing and your attitude disappears."

"Hell yea. She knows how to make daddy happy." And just like that, they were back to being happy again. Bi-polar ass motherfuckers.

****

After being at Fangora for almost four hours we decided the motherfucker wasn't gonna show. Eva was aggravated, and Niles and Kat couldn't wait to get home to fuck. I was pissed as well because this nigga wasted our time.

"Yo!" Some dude called out as we got to the car. We turned around and he stopped walking.

"What's up?" It's like he froze because he didn't move and no words left his mouth. None of us understood why until we looked over at my sister. She had a grin on her face, which meant she was doing something.

"He's about to tell us the guy had a change of plans and will contact you when he can meet up."

"Why you stop him though?" She tossed her purse in the car and went to him.

"This is why?" She pulled a little black pouch out his waist and opened it. My sister knew everything about a person, from them hiding shit to knowing if they had diseases before the person. Its like she could look at a person and know right away.

27

"What's that?" Kat asked.

"From the looks of it, I'd say it's some sort of serum; which kind? I won't know until we get to the house." We got in our cars and rushed over to her place.

"What about the guy?" Kat questioned. She may be like us but she's still in the dark about a lotta things.

"He'll be fine." Eva dropped her stuff on the table, pressed the button in her office that leads to a lab and went to work. We all sat there for an hour waiting to hear what was in the syringes.

"Looks like this is Mono and LCD."

"MONO! LCD!" All of us shouted at the same time. She pushed the liquid out each one and disposed of them in the small incinerator she had built inside. My sister designed her own house and had a lotta secret rooms, this being one of them.

"The two drugs combined are what vampires use now to find out if other people are the same. You inject the serum in the person and if they die, they're human. The dosage is too strong for a human to handle and kills them instantly. If they don't, they're vampires."

"Tha fuck?" I was mad as hell.

"Cal don't be upset because if this guy is from outta town he must be trying to see if we're legit."

"Ain't nobody gotta lie."

"You're right, but he may have run across people who did in the past. Actually, it's a good thing. He just tried it on the wrong people or should I say, was going to try." She smiled and all of us followed her out the room.

"What should we do?" Niles asked about meeting up with him if he called.

"You should meet up with him and I'm coming."

"Nah. If he thinks we crooked, I don't wanna be bothered."

"It's best if we do meet up with him because if he's this cautious he may do well on our team."

"A'ight. But if he turns out to be suspect, we making his ass disappear."

"You already know." Niles and I gave each other a pound and they left. He didn't possess the fairy powers we had but he's just as strong and powerful.

I told Eva I was staying the night and took my ass upstairs to the guest room. I couldn't help but think about the guy tryna stick us with those needles. Did he really think he'd get away with it? Whatever the case, we'll find out soon enough who this dude is.

Niles

"What's that all about?" Kat asked when we got home.

"Which part?" I put the keys on the kitchen counter, placed her on top of it and stood in between.

"About this guy wanting to know if y'all are real or not? Shouldn't he know if you found him?"

"Not necessarily." I unzipped her calf boots and tossed them on the floor, then did the same with her socks.

"People pretend to be one of us all the time, therefore; vampires concoct some sort of serum to help them figure it out."

"Really?" I lifted her leg.

"You have no idea the things we've seen growing up."

"Sssss." She silently moaned when I placed one of her toes in my mouth. I sucked on each of them the way she liked. Afterwards, I removed all her clothes and stared.

My wife was beautiful to me and it's no reason I cheated on her. Honestly, I figured because she was a white woman, she'd allow me to do whatever I wanted and still stick

31

around. I mean she wasn't turned yet, we both wanted kids and truth be told, I was in love with her.

In the beginning, she kept asking why she couldn't get pregnant knowing we were fucking all the time and unprotected. I couldn't tell her about me being a vampire yet and if I changed her, she wouldn't be allowed to have kids because vampires couldn't reproduce with each other. The person has to be fully human in order to make it happen unless you have the powers my cousins have.

I asked my cousins grandfather to give me the stuff to release my sperm so I could get her pregnant. Two days later we had sex, and two weeks after that, she became pregnant. However; my mom said I had to tell her because she wouldn't be pregnant long and the kids had to feed differently.

Shockingly, she wasn't upset, said she wanted more kids and then, to be turned like me. She didn't wanna be human and end up dying. Eventually, I changed her, married her and again, I cheated thinking she'd stick around now because vampires rarely ever get divorced but it happens.

One night I came home after being with another woman and she knew. Don't ask me how but she did. Kat had already packed up the kids and took them to her parents' house. She cursed me out like I've never been cursed out before and left my ass. A nigga was sick and vowed to do whatever necessary to bring my family home.

Long story short, the night before Kat told me she was coming back, I went out with my cousin Cal. We got so fucked up at the bar neither of us could drive home. Our dumb asses decided to fly because we'd get there faster. That had to be the dumbest decision we ever made. Both of us were flying into trees, houses and I hit a damn bus. By the time we got to my house, both of us were tore up and tryna heal.

Cal left not too long after and after fully healing, I went upstairs to shower. I laid in the bed only to be woken up by my wife giving me head or so I thought. She was doing her thing but I knew something was different because my wife always swallows and this specific night she didn't.

I looked down, saw the red hair and flipped. My wife and her twin were identical except for the hair color and Kat had a mole on the top of her eyebrow.

I hopped up out the bed, turned and backhanded the shit outta her sister Megan. I've never in my life hit a woman but she deserved it. I didn't care that her nose was broken. Who the fuck told her to come in my house and in my bedroom at that? I told that bitch if she ever told my wife I'd kill her.

I was happy my cousin was fucking her now because it kept her away. When I told him what she did, he promised to do her dirty in the bedroom and he did. I haven't watched the video but if the bitch ever come outta pocket I have leverage to use on her.

"Are you happy with me Niles?" Her head was tilted back and I was just about to dive in. I stopped, pulled her up and made her look at me.

"You are perfect for me Kat and I'm gonna continue making it up to you."

"I'm not asking because of the past Niles. I'm asking because I don't want us to ever separate so if it's ever anything

34

I'm doing wrong or not doing enough of; please tell me so I can fix it."

"Again; baby you are perfect for me." I pecked her lips, lifted her up and carried her to the roof. We had a big house and up here held a patio set and some other stuff she decorated it with. She loved being up here.

"Why are we up here?"

"Because you like when I make love to you under the moonlight."

"I love you Niles." I put her on the rooftop and laid her down. If she rolled the wrong way she'd fall off. We weren't worried because I'd catch her or she'd catch herself.

"I love you too Kat." I let my fangs drop and dove in.

"Shittttt." She moaned out and released everything she had. Just as I was about to remove my jeans, she stopped me and sat up.

"What's wrong?"

"Megan's at the door." She flew past me and went downstairs. I didn't even smell the bitch but I'm glad Kat did. I would never approve of anyone watching us have sex and it's no telling what the bitch is up to.

I took my time going down the steps until I heard yelling. When I stepped in the room, Kat had a robe on and her arms folded. Megan was on the couch crying her eyes out. I rolled mine and went in the kitchen. I felt Kat behind me and turned around.

"You smell good." Her juices were seeping out and I couldn't wait to taste her again. I let my hand go under her robe and slide up and down her bottom lips.

"Mmmmm. Baby stop. I need to talk. Sssss." I placed my finger in my mouth and sucked the juices off.

"We're definitely finishing later." She slid her hands in my jeans.

"HELL FUCKING NO!" I moved her hand and tossed the rest of my drink in the sink.

"I didn't ask yet."

"You know I can hear your thoughts."

"Why not Niles?"

"Because I don't like the bitch and she's sneaky as fuck."

"Baby don't say that."

"Fuck her. Matter of fact." I stormed out the kitchen and caught myself from moving fast. Megan had no idea who we were and it needs to stay that way. She can't be trusted.

Kat asked me a few times if I could find someone to change her and I objected every time. She's the type of person who finds shit out and tells. I couldn't and wouldn't risk our chances of survival on her.

"Get the fuck out." I gripped her arm and stood her up.

"Ouch Niles."

"Niles don't put your hands on her."

"Then she better get to fucking stepping. Why the fuck are you here at four in the morning anyway?"

"Baby, I was tryna tell you her boyfriend kicked her out and.-"

"Oh well. She better get a hotel, motel or stay in a rooming house because the bitch can't stay here."

"Niles we have plenty of room."

"Ain't no room for her and I'm not gonna tell you to leave again." I pushed her towards the door. My wife bounced upstairs mad as hell.

"What? You don't want her to know how well I sucked you off?" This is the exact type of shit I'm talking about. Here her sister is tryna help her, and all she wants to do is hurt her.

"I'm not worried about that shit but you should be."

"Why is that?"

"Because once she finds out, I doubt she'll ever fuck with you again. Now beat it bitch." I slammed the door in her face, locked it and flew up the steps.

"You can be mad all you want but ain't nobody staying here I don't like, and vice versa."

"Niles she has nowhere else to go."

"Not our problem." I shrugged and started taking my clothes off. She can stay with her mother but the two of them are like oil and milk. They don't mix either.

"But.-"

"You heard me Kat." She sat on the bed pouting. I didn't care about her acting like a brat. I meant what the fuck I

38

said about her not staying here and if she does on some sneaky shit, we're really gonna have a problem.

I stepped in the shower, washed up and came out to see her watching television and texting on her phone. I snatched it out her hand and of course it was Megan begging her to stay here. My wife told her no and we're a team so if I say no, it is what it is. This bitch had the nerve to say she'll sneak in at night and be gone in the morning. I see she's gonna be a got damn problem. I'ma need Caleb to send me that video ASAP.

Eva

"I don't wanna hear it Faine. You told the kids you'd be here. Where are you?" I was listening to another lame excuse from my baby daddy.

"I said, I'm outta town."

"You do know I can tell where you're at, right." He sucked his teeth. He hated my powers were so strong. I could tell his exact location at all times, when he was lying and even after he slept with someone and who she was.

"Tell them I had to cancel damn." He hung the phone up.

"It's ok mommy. We rather be here with you anyway." Selene sat on my lap and kissed my cheek.

At two years old in the human world and older in the vampire world, she's very smart. Outta all my kids, I see myself in her the most. My other kids have more of their fathers looks but thankfully none of them have his attitude.

"Yea but y'all were looking forward to being with him." She shrugged her shoulders. I could use my powers to make him spend time with them but I never believed in forcing a man to take care of their children. Kids are smarter than we think and mine know exactly what's going on and I hated that.

"What do you guys wanna do today?"

"Can we go see nana and pop pop."

"It's a long drive but we can if you want." She spoke of my grandfather and his wife Ambrosia, who I considered my grandmother.

My mother's, mother had to be killed because she was mad my grandfather didn't want her, and was working with another woman to kill them.

"Tell your sisters and brother we're leaving." She ran off and I started getting myself together. The kids loved going to their house because of the farm animals they had. I looked over at my phone going off and saw it was Caleb.

"Hey." I answered dryly.

"Let me guess. He backed out again." He could sense when I'm upset and even get in my head but when I dealt with Faine, I blocked everyone out because I didn't want them to see how he was. They knew but it's my problem, not theirs.

"Yup." I wanted to cry but refused to waste another tear on him. I wasn't crying for myself but for my kids. He's missing out on so much and they're the ones suffering. My son Faine Jr. asked me why his father hated them the other night. I swear my baby daddy wasn't shit.

"Fuck that nigga. Sis you know he'll be dead in seconds if you give me the word." Caleb hated him and so did Niles and everyone else in the family. It's one thing not to be with me but he's doing my babies dirty.

"If I didn't think the kids would be upset, I'd say go ahead." I glanced in the mirror and fixed my hair.

"What's up?"

"The dude called and we're gonna meet him tonight."

"Caleb I'm not about to go and his ass is a no show again." It's been two weeks since we went and I didn't feel like being stood up again.

"I told him that and he swore it won't be the same. I guess after dude told him you stripped him of the syringes, he wanted to meet us."

"Caleb if he doesn't show this time, fuck him."

42

"You got it sis. How long you gonna be at pop pop's?"

"The kids wanna go. I'll see if they'll keep them and come right back."

"A'ight. I'll see you around ten." We hung up and I put the kids in the car and prepared myself for this two-hour trip. Again, we could fly but my kids needed to be human as much as possible for when they get older.

We pulled up at my grandparents' house a little after three and they were at the door waiting. The kids hauled ass out the car and the first thing they asked was to play with those damn animals. I went inside with Ambrosia and sat in the kitchen while she made all of us something to eat.

"Honey, you can't let him get to you." I loved talking to her because she didn't judge and always knew what to say.

"I try not to but when it has to do with the kids, I wanna stab him in the heart."

"Do it then." My grandfather came in and hugged Ambrosia from behind. I loved their relationship as well. Between them, my parents and my aunt Irina and uncle Niles, it made me wonder why couldn't I have the same? Why did God place a loser in front of me?

"I can't." He gave me a look.

"I know I can but I'm thinking about the kids."

"Well no more complaining then. Let him deal with the questions and shit when they get older because they will ask." I nodded and ate the raw meat my grandmother made for me. I looked up and she was smiling at me.

"What?"

"You're a hopeless romantic just like your father." I had a grin on my face. I always did when someone spoke of him.

"I think tonight is the night." Ambrosia said and glanced over at my grandfather who was getting something out the fridge.

"For?" I questioned.

"For a new man to enter your life and sweep you off your feet." I busted out laughing.

"I'm serious Eva. You and Cal are the only two who aren't in some sort of relationship."

44

"Well, per my sister Lenore, no one can handle me." I used air quotes.

"No, this person who's gonna enter your life will be able to."

"Grandma, please tell me you didn't set me up on a blind date."

"I didn't but I do know of the person you guys are supposed to meet tonight and honey he is FINEEEEEEE!" My pop pop looked at her and she shrugged her shoulders.

"Wait until you see him."

"If he's fine, I definitely don't want him."

"We'll see sweetie but don't say I didn't warn you." I changed the subject because my grandmother was always tryna hook someone up.

They called her the matchmaker in the vampire world. Too bad my pop pop didn't listen when she told him Faine wasn't the right choice for me. I could've avoided a lot of unnecessary drama with him. If this is some sort of blind date, I'm positive this is her way of making it up to me.

****

"I'm gonna start having your ass drive your own shit to the club." Caleb barked because it took me forever to come out.

"Stop asking me to go places knowing I have to get the kids situated first."

"Eva don't play me. The kids can take care of themselves and you could've dropped them off and left. You stayed there running your mouth." I waved him off and pulled the visor down. I used the mirror to finish putting on my eyeliner.

"The line is long as usual."

"It's extra-long today because the guy *D* invited humans."

"Humans?"

"Yup. He had to make sure the club looked legit since it's in the middle of downtown. I mean what does it look like with only vampires inside?"

"Like no one is gonna get eaten." I said and we both laughed.

"Supposedly, every vampire entering has to take a shot of liquid Xanax." I shook my head. Xanax was used to quench the thirst of a vampire who'd be in the presence of humans. It suppressed their appetite for twelve hours. But don't be around when the shit wears off because they're like animals looking to eat.

"Let's get this over with. I'm already gonna miss Saturday night live." He sucked his teeth.

"You're not old sis, so live a little."

"I do Cal. I just hate being in clubs where people sweat all over each other and try to take the first whore home." He shook his head, hit the alarm on his car and took my hand in his. We walked across the street and security lifted the rope for us. He asked if Niles was coming and once we told him no; he put it down.

Evidently, him and Kat are going through something because he won't allow her sister to stay with them. To be honest, whether he let her suck his dick or not it's what's best. Sister or not, it's never a good idea to allow another woman to stay with you and your husband. Family are usually the first to fuck you over and, in this case, Megan is definitely that family member.

I met Megan through Kat and I knew right off the back she was a bad seed. She always had something smart to say when people spoke and a few times, I had to dig in her ass for thinking I was a bitch off the street. Her mother is no better, which is probably where she gets it from. I didn't care and told Kat we can be cool but she needs to keep her sister away from me before I kill her.

"Is he here?" I asked Cal and took a seat in the VIP section we were escorted to.

"Yea. He's in a meeting upstairs and he'll be down soon." I nodded and asked the waitress for a glass of the cancer drinks. They don't get me drunk but I do like to get tipsy. Cal asked the lady for two diabetes drinks. Its beer in the human world and I hated the taste of it. She walked away and as we waited I could hear all different types of thoughts.

One woman wanted to try out a black guy, while another wanted to have a threesome with her boyfriend. A vampire guy was whispering in some human's ear about taking her home and she wasn't trying to hear it. I shook my head because when it's a lotta people, the conversations and thoughts are hilarious.

My song by Cardi B and Khelani came on and I grabbed Cal's hand to dance with me. He hated to be on the dance floor but he would never allow anyone else to dance with me, so he had no choice. People were dancing and the chicks were shouting out the lyrics right along with me.

You don't hit my line no more, oh, ohhhhh, you don't make it ring, ring, ring. I can't keep this on the low, I wanttttt, you to make it ring, ring, ring.

The entire time we danced, I could feel someone watching me. The only thing is, I couldn't find the person. It's like they were breathing down my neck but their presence was unknown. I glanced around the club in search of the person without being suspicious because then Cal would think something was up. Then, I found him. *DAMN!!!!!*

Deray

I walked out the bathroom and sat at my desk. Tonight, I decided to invite humans to see how they interact with vampires. Usually, it's a member only club but I wanted to try something different. I was excited to see how many people actually showed up. It's not even about the money with me because I have a lot of it. I more so wanted to change the atmosphere of how humans portrayed us. Not that they'll know in here, but still.

I never planned on coming to this area but when someone mentioned the number of vampires that stayed here, it made sense. They moved around like humans and even though people may have been curious of who they were, no one ever questioned it. It's really a good thing because we wanted to be treated the same.

My ex is the other reason I'm here. We met in New York at a different club I opened and hit it off. She was human and even though I stayed up here, it didn't bother me one bit to drive and see her.

"Who the hell is that?" My boy Draven asked and pointed out the glass window of the office. I was going over paperwork to open more clubs all over the world. I wanted to make sure we had our own spots to hang out at.

At first, I sat there because he always found a new chick to look at. It wasn't until he mentioned she had yellow eyes. No vampire or human for that matter had yellow eyes and if they did, something was wrong with them.

I took my time walking over and grabbed the cup with my drink in it. He pointed to some woman who had on a mid-length navy blue dress. From behind you could tell she had an ass and I could see her pretty ass toes from the sandals she wore when she turned around.

I'm a foot man and if a bitch had ugly feet, I couldn't fuck with her on any level. What I look like dealing with a chick who had bear claws or deer hooves?

For some reason I couldn't take my eyes off her. I must say, she was mesmerizing. Her face had a glow to it, her eyes were definitely yellow and I sensed something different about her. She's a vampire for sure but something else is in her blood.

51

I noticed her stare up at me and mouth the words *DAMN.* I put my cup on the desk and made my way down to meet her. A few bitches stopped me on the way and I promised to speak with them later because right now, I needed to find the woman with yellow eyes.

She was no longer on the dance floor but the scent I'm assuming she left behind was strong as fuck. It was sweet and smelled like she was bathing in some sort of fruity soap. I didn't expect to see her in VIP with the Caleb dude I'm meeting. I'd hate for them to be dating because she bad as fuck. One thing I do know is, even if they are I'ma need to try her out.

As I made my way towards VIP, my phone went off but I ignored it. I can guarantee it's my pain in the ass ex and I don't feel like dealing with her at the moment. I told the bitch its over but clearly, she didn't get the memo.

"Hey boss." Security moved out the way and the smell grew stronger. I rushed over to her seat and made her stand.

"What are you?" I sniffed her neck and hair.

"GET THE FUCK OFF ME! ARE YOU CRAZY?"

She pushed me so hard, I left an indent in the wall. I went to move back and she put her palm out. My entire body froze. I started feeling hot, a small light came from her hand and the longer she had me frozen, the bigger it got.

"That's enough Eva." He smacked her hand and I was free.

"Tell him not to be running up on me. Who the hell do he think this is?"

"Bitch are you crazy?" She lifted her hand to do it again and Caleb stopped her.

"Yoooo!" Draven had a shocked look on his face.

"No disrespect bro but we didn't come here to get in no shit. We're waiting on *D* and we'll be gone."

"I am D."

"Oh shit. My bad. She's sorry about that." He put his hand out for me to shake.

"No the fuck I'm not Cal. I don't care who the hell he is. He don't be rushing me like we know each other." She folded her arms across her chest and I did the same.

"Calm your fucking attitude down." I barked and she looked at me.

"I don't give a fuck about the power you just used. You're in my fucking club and you need to show me some respect."

"Like you did when you ran up on me. Sniffing me like a got damn dog and shit."

"Oh fucking well."

"And why do you have a gold crown in your mouth? You're a vampire."

"I can do what I want. Why you all in my mouth anyway?" I could tell she was getting pissed.

"Why were you sniffing me?"

"I ain't never in my life met anyone with your smell."

"Oh, you're one of those guys who sleep with dirty bitches?"

"I didn't say a thing about fucking but I see where your head is at." I smirked and she rolled her eyes.

"Anyway Cal, I'll meet you downstairs." She walked away.

"Good and don't bring yo ass back up here until we're done talking."

"Fuck you."

"Not tonight ma. I have three women on deck."

"Dirty dick nigga."

"Vampires don't have dirty dicks." She gave me the finger and stormed outta VIP.

"I think she likes you."

"Sheeeitttt, if that's like, I'd hate to see the way she loves." He started laughing.

"I'm serious. She never gives men more than a *hello, get the fuck out my face and nigga, I'm gonna cut your dick off.* I'd say you're on a roll to get her to at least buy you a drink if y'all cross paths again." I turned around, leaned on the railing and stared at her. Shorty was bad as hell and whatever she's mixed with makes me wonder if there's more out here like her.

"Who is she to you?" He stood next to me drinking his beer.

"My twin."

"No shit!"

"Yea, its four of us in the first litter my parents had. She and I are the closest." I continued staring at her and noticed some guy walking towards her.

"I know this bitch is one of them because she has yellow eyes." I heard and watched as the man started digging under his shirt. How the hell did a hunter get in here?

"I'll be right back."

"LOOK OUT!" Someone shouted and this nigga pulled out a knife. He charged at Eva and she turned around at the same time he got close.

POOF! She let a ball of light hit him and that motherfucker was on the ground in ashes.

The music stopped and everyone stood there in amazement. She flicked her wrist and somehow a song came on that sounded like jazz. The human's eyes were turning colors and a few seconds later, the regular music came on and it's like no one remembered what happened.

"Let's go." I snatched her up and made her walk up to my office. She talked shit and I told her if she even thought about freezing me again, when I'm free I was gonna creep in her house at night and fuck the shit outta her.

She started talking more shit but I bet she didn't do it. I closed the door when her brother walked in and paced the floor. Draven must've gotten caught up in her spell because he wasn't up here.

"What the fuck was that?"

"That's nothing. This office is nice." She walked around looking at the pictures on the wall.

"Hell no. What did you do down there?"

"I just killed a man, erased everyone's memory of what they saw and you snatched me up. That reminds me. How are you able to remember? The spell is supposed to work on everyone."

"That mind compulsion shit don't work on me."

"And why is that?"

"I learned how to block my mind when someone does it."

"Did anyone ever tell you, you're an asshole?"

"All the time, now back to you. What are you?"

"Stop focusing on me and worry about this war we have coming. Are you in or not?" She rolled her neck and stood in my face.

"Can you give us a minute?"

"Yup." Her bother stepped out. I waited for the door to close and moved in closer to her. I put my nose in the crook of her neck again and smelled her entire body. I smiled when my head was below her waist.

"I turn you on." I stood and lifted her face to stare at me. I could smell her juices through her clothes.

"The liquor has me horny and all these men in here could be a candidate for tonight." I pushed her against the wall and forced my tongue down her throat. She accepted me and wrapped her arms around my neck. My dick began rising and she knew it.

"I turn you on." She moved away and pointed.

"You do. Now what? We fucking?" She smiled, grabbed her things and went to the door.

"Not at all. What type of woman do you think I am?"

"Then why go through all that?"

"I can pleasure myself tonight to you D."

"Fuck that! Right now is the perfect time." She had me brick hard by now and I needed a release.

"You want me D?"

"Can't you tell?"

"Then make me want you. Your first impression was horrible. This isn't the way I allow any man to date me." She opened the door and disappeared. How the hell did they come here for a meeting and we end up almost fucking?

I sent a text to her brother and told him we'd have to meet up another time but I'm down to be on their team. If she has those type of powers then I definitely see us winning this war.

****

"You're not into it Deray." The chick complained about me fucking her and her friends. Not only are they humans but freaky as hell, which is why I'm always fucking them.

"Y'all finish up and go." I got out the bed, threw my clothes on and grabbed my stuff.

"Deray what the hell is going on? You've never left us."

"I got some things on my mind. You gonna finish or what? If not, I'm about to turn this key in." I showed the hotel key and waited for an answer.

"I'm leaving."

"Why?"

"Because he's the one with the dick and if he ain't supplying it, then why would we stay?" Karen said and Latoya followed suit.

The only one still sitting there is Nicole who had the best pussy outta the three. The only thing I wasn't feeling about her is the attitude and the fact she claims to be pregnant. I know it ain't mine if she is but I definitely lost respect for her. Who the hell sleeps with other men with a baby in her stomach?

"Deray, where are you going?" She came running over to me naked and all. Karen and Latoya were shaking their heads and getting dressed.

"What I tell you about questioning me?" I started getting angry and that's one thing you don't wanna do. Karen witnessed me black out one time we were out chilling. I had to erase her memory just so she wouldn't tell anyone.

"Nicole back up."

"No fuck that. We come running whenever you want. Fuck in every position possible and let you and your niggas run trains on us. The least you can do is respect our presence and time." I dropped my keys, walked up on her and watched as her body started smoking.

"What's going on? Why am I burning up?" Karen and Toya stared at me and I wasn't doing a damn thing.

"Oh my God! How is your arm on fire?" They started trying to put it out and still, I stood there staring. I was able to burn people up with my powers. It gave me a headache afterwards but it's still fun to do.

"You know if she burns you have to kill the other two." I heard in my head and broke the stare to turn around. No one was there but I knew her voice from anywhere. The question is how the hell did she get inside my head? No one has been able

61

to do that since I was a kid. I grabbed my stuff and rushed to the door.

"Don't forget to erase what happened?" I heard again and turned to see the women trying to put the fire out. I was in such a rush to leave I almost forgot.

I left the hotel and almost had a few accidents. How did she do it? I asked her the same question over and over in my head but she refused to answer or maybe she didn't hear me. Whatever the case, I have to see her again. Who in the hell is she and where did she come from?

Eva

"Sssss." I silently moaned in my bed as I pleasured myself with thoughts of this Deray guy. He was so got damn sexy to me.

I figured out a way to get in his head that same night. I could see through his eyes and there were three women performing sexual acts amongst each other. They attempted to get him but he got up and left them hanging. I couldn't stop laughing when he set Nicole's stupid ass on fire. Not only is she sleeping with him and other women, she tried the pregnancy thing on him too. What's wrong with her? Is she really that desperate to have a child?

After meeting him two weeks ago, he stayed on my mind; literally. I mean every now and then I'd sneak in his head to see what he was doing and sometimes he caught me because I'd say something out loud. He didn't care and told me on plenty of occasions to stop playing shy and go out with him. Talking to him this way is better than texting if you ask me. I didn't have to worry about anyone screenshotting our conversation that's for sure.

Deray was very confident in his appearance and he should be. He had to be at least six foot or taller. I loved his caramel complexion and his demeanor is something I've never dealt with. He didn't care about the power I had and still had me following his directions. Is he the man my grandmother said I'm destined to meet and if so, I can see us having wild sex all the time? We wouldn't be good in a relationship because I'm the boss and it's gonna stay that way.

"Mmmmm." I continued pleasing myself and laid there outta breath once I finished. It's been a while since I slept with someone and the feeling was just what I needed. I usually reminisce off the sex Faine and I had but not this time. This Deray guy had all my attention.

Just as I started dosing off my phone rang. I didn't notice the number and answered anyway.

"Hello."

"Open your door." His tone was rude but what I really wanna know is how did he find out where I lived.

"I'm in for the night sir."

"Open this fucking door or I promise to kick it down."

"Oh my. You're very aggressive. Now like I said, I'm in.-" My words were cut short when I heard tapping at my balcony window. I turned and he was standing there smoking something. I grabbed my robe and walked over.

"You do know this is breaking and entering."

"Not until I break this glass and it's exactly what I'm gonna do if you don't open this door." The second I turned the doorknob; my body flew to the other side of the room with him standing in my face. I could feel his breath on my neck and then he started that sniffing shit again.

"Ok, this sniffing is for animals. You're gonna have to stop."

"I see you played with yourself." He moved his fingers down and I smacked his hand away.

"I see you had a bunch of thots in your hotel room."

"Yea about that. How the hell are you getting in my head? And why you taking your time going out with me?" He moved away and I couldn't help but stare at his tattoos. He had a few piercings I didn't notice at the club and his body was fucking immaculate.

"I can do a lot of things and I don't reveal my secrets."

"The reason we haven't gone out yet is...."

"Is because you're a man who enjoys sleeping with many women and I've dealt with that already. I'm not tryna do it again so we can be cordial with one another for the time being." He stared at me and for a minute, I felt embarrassed under his gaze.

"Don't be shy now."

"I'm not shy."

"Then why are you grabbing the blanket to wrap around you?

"Because I have a man in my room, I don't know staring at me."

"You love it otherwise you would've used your powers to kick me out by now; which we both know you can do." He moved closer to me.

"What is it about you that has me unfocused?" He ran his hand down the side of my face.

"I don't know what you mean." I moved away but he came behind me.

"No woman in this world has made me stop fucking other women or even been able to get in my head." His hand went in my hair and once again we engaged in a kiss. I felt his hands on my shoulders as he removed the robe and had me stand their naked.

"Got damn you're sexy as fuck."

"Thank you very much but you gotta go." I snatched my robe off the ground and pushed him toward the door.

"I ain't going nowhere."

"Deray, we're supposed to go out on dates and stuff first. You're trying to skip all that."

"Hell yea, I am." He locked the doors in the room, scooped me up, cradled me against his chest and laid me down gently on the bed. He kissed my body from head to toe and I knew if I didn't make him leave we'd go further.

"We can't do this. I'm not a ho and oh my gawddddddd." I damn near screamed out when he clamped down on my pussy. He was sucking the hell outta my clit and fingering me at the same time. I was in heaven but it wasn't right. I didn't even know this man and I'm allowing him to do sexual things to me.

"If I swallow ain't nothing gonna happen to me, is it?" I wanted to smack him but he curved his finger inside, and bit down on my clit again. I came harder than I ever did. My body was shaking and I thought he'd get up but he continued and had me screaming his name.

"That's some good ass pussy." My arm was over my eyes as I tried catching my breath. He kissed up my body and our tongues danced together once again.

"I'm good Eva." I threw him against the wall, stripped him outta his clothes, wrapped my mouth around his long and humongous dick and gave him the business.

"Oh Fuckkkkk!" He was fucking my face, moaning and grabbing my hair.

"Shitttttttt. Got damn." I sucked all he had out and stood.

He stared in my eyes and for a moment, the two of us were lost in one another. Neither of us said a word and it's like these feelings came outta nowhere. All of a sudden, I wanted him to be my man. *What the hell is going on?*

His phone rang and instead of answering it, he pulled my body into his. I felt his man growing, jumped in his arms and waited for him to enter me.

"Ahhh shit." It definitely hurt going in but it felt good once I started popping up and down on him.

His hands squeezed my ass and he pushed me down harder. I know he wanted to make me feel him and trust me I did. He put my back to the wall, held both of my hands above my head and thrusted inside harder. We were now kissing one another aggressively and fucking the shit outta each other. Unfortunately, he stopped for some reason.

"Eva, maybe we should wait."

"I don't want to." I grabbed his neck and started kissing him again.

"I'm saying. I didn't expect it to be so damn good." He was still sliding in and out as he spoke.

"Then why do you wanna stop?" I looked at him and again, we got lost for a minute. *What the hell was going on between us?*

"I'm not sure we're right for each other and say what you want. but I don't want another nigga or vampire having this feeling."

"Deray just fuck me."

"Nah, we gotta stop." He let me down and I instantly caught an attitude.

"Eva?"

"Fuck you Deray. Get out."

"Look, I've never met anyone like you and.-"

"Save it and GET THE FUCK OUT!" I shouted and his eyes turned red.

"Who the fuck you talking to?" He had me by my throat against the wall.

"You. Get off me." I pushed him away and watched as he fell into the dresser.

"What I tell you about doing that shit?" He charged me and I fell into the wall. The indent was bad but I didn't care.

"Are you serious?" I went to freeze him and he moved out the way.

"Get yo childish ass the fuck over here." He yanked me by the back of the hair almost making me fall.

"Acting like a got damn brat because I'm tryna take it slow."

"Take it slow my ass. How you fuck me and stop in the middle? You're childish. Take your ass home." My hand went across his face and he got even angrier.

"This is what you want Eva?" He tossed me on all fours on the bed, and spread my legs as far as they can go, with his other hand wrapped around my throat. In one quick thrust, he entered.

"AHHHHHHH!" I screamed when he stuck his big dick in my ass. He pushed my face in the bed and dog fucked me. I was cumming so much my eyes were rolling and I started feeling things I never did with Faine. But how, when we didn't know each other?

"I swear Eva from here on out it's me and you." He smacked my ass and kept switching from my ass to my pussy.

"Whatever Deray." I said it to piss him off. He went faster and I had to do the same.

"Yea ma. Fuck that's sexy." He now had me on my back with my legs on his shoulders cumming on his dick.

"Fuck. Fuck. Fuck. I'm about to cum." He moaned out and I pushed him off.

"I want all your cum in my mouth Deray. Cum for me baby." And just like that, he gave me so much I could've probably filled a cup up. He fell on the bed and passed the hell out. That's how you put a man to bed.

I went in the bathroom, cleaned myself up, washed his dick off and went to sleep. Four straight hours of fucking with no breaks is exactly what I needed.

Deray

"I hope whatever you and that bitch did was worth it." My ex said when I made it to my house. I kicked the bitch out but for some reason she's still here.

"Trust me. It definitely was." I tossed my keys on the table and walked up the stairs in my mansion to shower. I was hoping this bitch wouldn't come in nagging, however, I couldn't be so lucky.

"So you're just gonna disrespect me by coming in after fucking some ho?"

I let the water beat down on me as I reminisced about how Eva threw it on my ass. In all the years I've been a vampire and even the short time as a human when I did fuck, I've never encountered pussy as good as hers.

I know men say this one is the best or that one is, but the feeling Eva gave me when I was inside her was different. It's like she put a spell on my dick and it craved her the second I pulled out. And let's not even discuss to two moments we had with each other. If I didn't know any better, I'd say we imprinted on one another and that means ain't no other nigga ever fucking her.

I woke up still in her bed and rolled over to see she wasn't there. I thought about taking a shower but I needed to get as far away as possible. Unfortunately, that didn't happen because Eva came strolling in the room naked. She gestured for me to follow her and the two of us fucked in the pool, on the lawn chairs and brought it back to the bedroom. Four days of being under her, had a nigga stuck and unsure of the feelings surfacing.

Then, I come home assuming I'll have peace and quiet and time to think about what's going on and this bitch here. Don't get me wrong, I loved her at one point and planned on marrying her but she can't be trusted. I found out not only was she cheating but stealing money out the safe to fund her little rendezvous. Like how you taking my money to fuck another nigga?

When I confronted her on it, she tried to throw it on me because she knew I was cheating. It's not my fault she decided to stick around. Women called and told her about the sexscapades we had and I promised to stop but the pussy was calling me, so I took it.

I think once she accepted it the first two times I kept doing it knowing she wouldn't leave. However; once she sought out revenge it was a wrap. I'm not about to claim no bitch who's fucking people I know. I tossed her ass out and somehow, she's back.

"I'm not disrespecting you because I kicked yo ass the fuck out." I started washing up and listened to her bitch and complain about me not loving her.

"You finished?" I grabbed the towel from the rack, dried off and stepped in the bedroom.

"Deray this isn't what I signed up for. You promised to take care of me and..."

"And I did but you dipped out and found someone else. Why can't he take care of you?"

"We wouldn't be in this situation if you never cheated first."

"I didn't take you as someone who'd seek revenge." I grabbed some boxers out and clothes to throw on. I had to meet with Caleb to figure out who's coming for us. The two times we were to meet up something stood in the way.

"Deray please don't do this." I turned around and she was crying. At one point in my life, I was in love with her but with the constant nagging and being lazy, I began to stray.

The first time she caught me out there, I felt like shit because she cried for days. I stayed around her every day to make sure she didn't leave. A year went by and I was caught again. That time she moved out and I made her come home. I didn't cheat anymore after that and stayed as faithful as a church nigga. I came home every night and did any and everything to make up for the hurt I caused her.

I don't know what happened but some bitch saw her and lied saying we were together and my girl believed her. From then on it was always accusations and I couldn't take it so I went out and did what she said.

She knew every time too because I'd smell like another woman, or wouldn't come home for days at a time. Yet and still, she stuck around. I told her on plenty of occasions she could reside here until she got a job and moved on her own.

I'm barely here so it didn't bother me until she started fucking other men. In my eyes, one of them should be funding her apartment or something but nope she brought her ass here.

"We're no good for each other and you know it. Now I gave you plenty of time to find a place and you didn't. Yo ass haven't even went out to look for a job." I felt her hands around my waist as I put my boxers on and then they slid inside.

"What you doing yo?"

"Deray neither of us are going anywhere so let's make up like we always do and move forward." She dropped her clothes and my man grew. I'm not even gonna lie; my ex had some good pussy too but this is not gonna happen.

"God dammit." She squatted down and took me in her mouth.

"I gotta goooo..." I tried to get out but she started juggling my balls and that was it. I lifted her up, threw her on the bed and forced myself in.

"Go slow Deray. You know I have to get used to you again." This is the only problem fucking humans. They couldn't take all the dick like a female vampire could. Only half could fit in a human, where a female vampire could take all of it.

"I love you Deray." She whispered after we finished. I didn't respond because my phone was going off and my feelings were no longer there. I looked at my phone and it was a message from Caleb asking where I was.

I hopped up, re showered and hurried out the house. It was after eight so I may as well expect a long night since the meetings at the club. I sent a message to my ex and told her ass, she better be gone and not to come back.

****

After three hours of discussing the pros and cons of this so-called war, we were all on the same page. We had ammunition and thousands of people waiting in the wind for the word.

The war we keep discussing isn't so much with regular humans. We're talking about the fake ass, wannabe vampire hunters. You know the people who make up their own cult and have all these dumb ass followers. I mean we have a lot of them too but something about this specific group is dangerous. They supposedly have stuff that can kill us on impact. I'm not sure it's possible being immortal and all but we had to be prepared for anything.

"What's up with you and my sister?" Caleb asked and his cousin Niles turned to listen.

"As of right now, nothing."

"Four days of fucking isn't nothing." Niles said and sipped the drink out his cup.

"Damn bro. How y'all know?"

"Well he and his sister are very close and he tells me, therefore we're all besties." He said and all of us laughed.

"Eva good peoples and I've never had a woman make me feel the way she did in only four days."

"What you mean?"

"The two of us only wanted sex but in the midst of it all something happened."

"I know good and got damn well y'all didn't imprint on each other."

"It's exactly what I think happened; with me anyway. I mean she had me so stuck I didn't wanna leave. I don't want another nigga around her and I already staked claim on her."

"Damn nigga you sound strung out."

"Whatever." I wasn't about to admit to what may be the truth.

"Can we imprint on each other if both of us been in love with other people?"

"If neither of you had a connection with your previous lovers than absolutely. We all know once you imprint on someone, it won't happen again and as far as I know in our world, it hasn't." I thought about what they were saying and decided to have a talk with my grandfather and then Eva. If I imprinted on her, how could I have sex with my ex? My dick ain't even supposed to get hard for another woman.

"There she is."

"Who?" They both stared over the railing at the club. It wasn't as packed as usual but there were a lotta people here.

"Eva."

"Where?"

"She just got out the car. She'll be in."

"What the hell?" Cal shouted and they looked at me.

"I can smell her."

"Smell her?"

"Yes. It's how I found where she was sitting the first time y'all showed up here. Her scent invaded my nostrils and still does every time."

"Yea. This nigga imprinted on her." Niles laughed and sat back down at the table over- looking the dance floor.

A few seconds later, Eva stepped in looking like a million bucks. Her glow was perfect and so was the red bodycon dress. Her feet were showing and the smile on her face after looking up at me only solidified us belonging together. Anytime two people can make each other smile the way we do, I'd say it's a match.

I nodded as security looked my way to make sure it's ok for her and the friend to enter. I wasn't sure who the friend was until she got up close and regretted letting her in. Thankfully, she didn't say two words to me and sat in Niles lap.

She must be his girl because the second she sat, they were going at it like teenagers.

"Hey sexy." Eva smiled and moved in closer.

"Hey."

"Can I come over later?"

"I'm all yours right?" I grabbed her waist.

"Hell fucking yea." I used my finger to lift her chin. The second I parted her lips and our tongues met, she smacked fire from my ass.

"Get your fucking hands off me." I was pissed because not only did she smack me, she started causing a scene.

"Tha fuck is wrong with you?"

"You're all mine right? No bitch can fuck you like me, right? I guess you found one because you smell just like her." FUCK! I forgot I slept with my ex. I didn't even think about tryna cover up her scent because she's not a vampire and I figured with me taking a shower, it would've been covered like always.

"Eva." I reached out for her.

"Don't tough me Deray." She tried to walk away and I ran in front of her, well flew.

"How dare you sleep with another woman the same day you slept with me?"

"It wasn't like that. My ex was at my house, I told her to leave and..."

"No wonder I couldn't hear you when you left."

"Why do you keep tryna get in my head?" She ignored me.

"What did you use to cover yourself?" I ran my hand down my face.

The soap and shampoo I used is to make sure no one can get in my head. I don't know how she did it the first night we met and couldn't earlier.

"Then you kiss me knowing she got a damn disease. Are you tryna kill me?"

"Say what now?"

"Oh, I forgot. You won't know she has a disease for two more days because it hasn't run all the way through yet."

"Eva lets go." Her brother said.

83

"Wait a minute Cal. Let me fill him in real quick on some things." She wiped the lone tear falling down her face. We had to imprint on one another if she already crying over me.

"Over the last few days somehow I imprinted on you Deray." I knew it.

"Don't ask me how or why but I did. I asked my grandmother how is it possible after not knowing you and she said, it's because you're the one. The one I've been waiting for. The reason no other man could get close to me." I tried to speak but she cut me off again. I wanted to tell her I felt the same but how could I when I fucked my ex?

"Now granted, it's only been a few days but once you imprint you know as well as I that's it. No one else can take your place but guess what I know? Imprint or not, I will not tolerate a man cheating on me after one day of asking me to be his woman."

"I fucked up Eva. Let me make it up to you."

"Damn right you fucked up." She went to leave and turned around.

84

"Oh, and the disease she gave you doesn't have a cure. You better be happy you're a vampire because otherwise you'd be on a lotta medications for the rest of your life."

"What?"

"Yea your ex has HIV." She stormed off and I caught her at the front door. I don't care who saw me fly across the dance floor.

"Eva let me talk to you."

"It's over Deray."

"Stop saying that." I felt my anger building.

"It is and you can't force me to be with you."

"The hell if I can't." I snatched her up by the arm and flew across the parking lot.

"Deray stop this. You're making it obvious of what we are."

"Fuck those people." I took her face in my hands.

"I imprinted on you too Eva and I'm sorry for messing up. I don't know what happened because I thought once you imprint on someone your body belonged to only them.

Somethings not right ma can't you see?" She didn't say anything. I heard some yelling and turned my head.

"Who the fuck is that?" She turned around and I saw a few people coming in our direction.

"We gotta get outta here Eva."

"What? Who are they?"

"Vampire killers."

"They can't kill us."

"Eva until we know what they're working with we can't take any chances. Let's go." I grabbed her hand and just as we were about to leave she hit the ground.

"Oh shit." I saw a stream of light leaving out her body which should be blood. What the fuck is she?

I summoned Caleb and Niles in my head and told them I'm taking Eva to her house and to meet me. As I was leaving, I heard gunshots, people screaming and pure chaos going on. I guess the war is about to start because I'm damn sure gonna find out who the fuck these people are.

Caleb

The sound of flesh tearing and the sight of blood pouring out always gave me an adrenaline rush. Staring down at these dead people who shot my sister with something, gave me a sense of peace being they won't be able to hurt her again. Unfortunately; they're more out there like them.

I glanced around the parking lot and people were watching and recording on their phones. I flicked my wrist and watched as everyone stood there frozen.

I summoned the clean-up vampire people to come dispose of these bodies and told Niles and Kat to get over to Eva's. They refused to leave me and I appreciated it but I needed them there to let my mother know who Deray is because right now, she's cursing him out and asking tons of questions. My grandparents are on their way and would've been there first but Eva's kids are at their house.

After the street was cleaned up, I took the spell off and made sure all the memories were erased. However; one woman stood out because she started coming towards me. I used my shirt to wipe the remaining blood off my face and tossed it in my car. I wasn't worried about her seeing it because I'd erase her memory too. When we were face to face, she smiled.

"You cleaned up pretty fast." She glanced around the parking lot.

"I don't know what you're talking about."

"Besides the blood being a dead giveaway that a murder of some kind possibly happened, I saw the entire thing." I wasn't admitting to anything.

"Can you elaborate because I still have no clue what you're talking about." I folded my arms and listened to her tell me how we ripped those people to shreds and disposed of them.

"Who are you again?"

"I'm Zurie and I came here looking for my cousin Deray. He mentioned something about a war and if I wanted in."

"And do you?"

"Absolutely. These same types of people killed my parents."

"How were you able to witness anything that happened here?"

"Deray taught me a while ago how to get past the mind compulsion thing. It really is stupid for vampires to use on others but I could see how it's necessary at times." She shrugged and asked if Deray were inside.

I told her no but she could call him and go from there. I don't know this chick and anyone can say they're related. She's definitely a vampire but again, it don't mean shit to me. Unless her cousin introduces us, she's still a vampire off the street in my eyes.

After she left and I made sure all the memories were erased, I raced to my sister's house to find everyone there; including Kat's sister. They were outside talking but the fact she's even here is weird because Megan and Eva don't speak. There's no animosity between them anymore and they're never around one another.

I gave them the head nod, went in and closed the door. I sent a message in my head to Kat telling her not to even think about letting her sister in. She understood and told me she's in the process of leaving anyway.

"How is she?" I asked my grandmother Ambrosia.

"She was hit with an arrow that must've been dipped in holy water and contaminated blood." Contaminated blood is a quick way to kill vampires but a dead person's blood is the deadliest thing out there to us. Before you ask, there is a difference.

Contaminated blood is still alive if that makes sense. It means the person is alive and infected. A dead person's blood is just that; dead. Therefore; if it gets into our system it shuts a vampire down and within an hour or two, they'll be dead as well.

"WHAT?" Everyone screamed out.

"Whoever's the leader of this group has to know things about vampires in order to know this could put one down."

"Is she gonna die?" Deray asked and you could see concern and sadness on his face.

"Fortunately, you got her here in time so no. However; her body is different from everyone else's so it's going to take a lot more time to heal."

"Why is that?" Ambrosia stared at him.

"When did you meet Eva?"

"A few of days ago. Why?"

"You're the guy."

"Huh?" He was just as lost as the rest of us.

"I told her she'd meet a guy and he'd sweep her off her feet. She didn't believe me but told me earlier today I had to meet you because she thinks I was right." A grin came across his face.

"Kharis, this is the guy we talked about the other day." My mom waved her off and put her head down next to Eva's hand. My father was in the bed with her and refused to get up.

"Can I ask you a question?" Deray turned to Ambrosia.

"Sure."

"If we imprinted on one another, how was I able to sleep with another woman?" My father sat up.

"You cheated on her already?"

91

"It wasn't like that and..."

"That is weird. Are you sure y'all imprinted?" My grandfather asked.

"Positive."

"The only person who can do that is an elder. They have the ability to put a cloak over you so once you imprint, the true love and happily ever after part gets blocked."

"Meaning?"

"If you two are meant to be together, the cloak blocked the spell of you not being allowed to sleep with other women. Eva's even allowed to lie with another man."

"Not a chance in hell will that ever happen." Everyone busted out laughing.

"When Eva wakes up, you have to get her to find the spell to break the cloak over you. If she can, then the imprint process will be complete. If not, every woman you go around will get you aroused and you will fail victim to them." My grandmother said.

"Eva won't stick around if you're wondering." My father chimed in and no one said a word. Who in the hell would wanna interfere with the person my sisters supposed to be with?

****

Two days went by and Eva had yet to open her eyes. Deray and my parents haven't left her side and the kids were back and forth from here and my grandparents.

I had to grab him some clothes from the store because he was too nervous about leaving the house and getting caught up with other women. I didn't blame him because once you get on Eva's bad side you can forget it.

"How much longer before mommy opens her eyes?" My niece Selene asked walking in the room. Deray moves out the way and offered her the chair he was in. He gestured me with his eyes to step outside.

"Your grandparents never answered my question."

"And what's that?" I walked in the kitchen.

"What are y'all?"

"They're called Faepyre's." My grandmother on my father's side answered for me. Honestly, I wasn't gonna tell him. It was Eva's job to do so.

"What the hell is that?"

"A vampire mixed with fairy."

"Hold up." He had his index finger and thumb on his forehead like he was thinking.

"Eva is part vampire and part fairy? How is that even possible? Fairies and vampires don't even get along."

"To make a long story short, I've always been a fairy and never told anyone. Cassius, who is my husband had cancer and was dying. He asked his best friend Ambrogio to change him so he can live as long as us. Once he turned, Cassius asked for Ambrogio's daughter to change Caleb so he can stay alive too. So when Caleb had kids with Kharis they were mixed with the two. Got it."

"I think so." He paced the kitchen.

"Is that where the light comes from?"

"Yup but she has other powers because of the mixture. And she's a nerd so her ass stayed in the library teaching herself new things too."

"Wow."

"Yea it's pretty weird." My grandmother walked out and Deray went back in the room with Eva.

I told my parents I'd be back because Niles needed help with the kids. Besides Selene, Eva's other kids were over there and he claims it's too many. I tried to get in touch with Faine but his punk ass wouldn't answer the phone or in his head. I hated my sister was responsible for changing him. His time was definitely coming.

Faine

"Why do you keep putting off seeing your kids?" The bitch Megan asked. She and I been fucking for a minute now.

"Why the fuck you wanna know?"

"I don't. I'm asking because if you're still in love with her, wouldn't that be your chance to see her?" She rolled her naked body on top of mine.

"Eva will never take me back so it really doesn't matter if I'm still in love with her or not."

"How do you know?" I didn't respond.

Eva and I were destined to be together; per her grandfather. It's the reason he chose her to change me. However; Eva's a woman of many powers and an attitude outta this world. I loved her with everything I had but, in my eyes, nothing was good enough and no man would ever be worth anything to her. She's used to getting her way with all the men in the family, and boy did she want it that way forever.

Eva expected me to do everything she wanted, and nothing I wanted. I think the only time we were compatible was in the bedroom and even then, she tried to take control. I don't know what type of man she was looking for or dreamed of, but I damn sure ain't him.

As far as my kids go, I love them to death. Selene is more like her mother but I still loved her the same. It's not like I don't wanna see them but as petty as it sounds, I really do love Eva and if she took me back, I'd go running and spend more time with them. I didn't wanna be around them and couldn't have her. Call me what you want, but it is, what it is.

The real reason she left me is because of my cheating ways. But how the hell was I supposed to know once you change, your sexual appetite increases by like a thousand? Don't get me wrong, Eva gave it to me whenever I wanted but when I went out, it's like the women knew I was a newbie. They'd throw themselves at me and instead of fighting the urge, I went along with it. I lost a great woman in the process of fucking. A very controlling woman; but great nonetheless.

"You asking me all these questions but ain't you cheating on yo nigga?"

"Fuck him. He's out there screwing all these different women and expects me to sit home."

"Vampires do that." She pushed herself off me.

"Vampires?" She looked confused.

"Don't tell me you didn't know Deray's a vampire."

"Hell no I didn't. Shit, I thought it was a myth. No wonder I never got pregnant." I laughed.

"Megan there's a way he can get you pregnant."

"But he's dead."

"Why do humans think vampires are dead?"

"Ugh, because they're cold and have no soul."

"Was Deray cold?"

"No but.-"

"Exactly. Megan, listen to yourself. Do you really believe anyone could walk this earth without a soul? And vampires have a heart because it's the exact place humans aim for when trying to kill us."

"Us?" She hopped off the bed.

"Yea us. And why you get up?" I sat against the headboard.

"Because you're dead."

"When I'm fucking you do I feel dead?"

"Well no but..."

"Ok then. Humans made up the theory about vampires not being alive. We all know it's not true because your man is one and so am I."

"How can you go outside and if y'all can have kids why don't he and I have one?"

"This ain't twilight Megan. Certain vampires can go outside and no one will know the difference. The reason our bodies aren't cold before you ask is because the blood we drink, warms us up. The more we drink, the longer our body stays at room temperature."

"Wow!"

"As far as kids, he must didn't want any with you because it's definitely possible." She had the nerve to catch an attitude with me and started getting dressed.

"I'm going to find out why he didn't tell me." I rushed to the door and her mouth dropped. I've never showed her my moves until now.

"If you mention this, he will kill you."

"WHAT?"

"No human is supposed to know so if you wanna stay alive, keep the shit to yourself."

"I don't know Faine. This is big. They're people out there offering rewards to turn them in." I snatched her by the arm.

"I can guarantee you won't make it alive to even tell them."

"Is that a threat?"

"More like a promise." I pushed her out the hotel room and slammed the door in her face.

I hated I never let Eva show me how to do mind compulsion. I didn't feel the need to ever do it on anyone.

I thought about going after Megan and changed my mind. I had to sit back and think of what to do. It's not like I can even tell anyone I mentioned it to her because they'll kill me. The first rule of thumb is to never tell a human what we are. I gotta do better.

****

"Are you sure this is what you wanna do?" Bob asked and passed me a glass of water that I didn't drink.

"Positive."

"Can I ask why are you doing this? Most people believe we're some sort of cult who are following myths."

"Well Bob, I think we can all agree vampires shouldn't be allowed to reside amongst us. I mean, what if they get angry and tear one of our children to shreds or other family members. I don't believe our streets are safe." I was sitting in a meeting these vampire hunters were holding.

The night they shot Eva outside the club, I followed Bob in his car. He's the only one who was able to escape somehow. Anyway, he rushed home and I parked behind him. You could tell he was nervous when he stepped out his car but I got out mine too. I walked up and asked what did he use to shoot the woman and at first, he pretended not to know what I was talking about.

After telling him I wanted to know because vampires were on my street and I was scared for my family, he took me in the shed behind his house. He had an entire fake lab back there. There were tons of bottles, syringes and even needles that you put the stuff in and load it in a gun. This man was ready to murder all vampires.

Long story short, we ended up exchanging numbers and I called him here and there to portray a fake friendship. A few weeks later he had me attend some meeting and it took everything in me not to kill the people there. They were talking mad shit about vampires and it was all false. It didn't matter to me because the only thing I wanted was the antidote to kill them.

Last week Bob let me watch him make it and I've been cloning the shit ever since. My house had as much of those bottle as he did. Now I'm waiting for the right time to use it on these motherfuckers.

In the process, Bob and his boys have been creeping up and killing some. I'm not sure how they're doing it but that's the next question for, the next meeting because I had some things to do. It's just a matter of time before this war gets started and I can't fucking wait. Of course, I'll be playing both sides. That way they won't know what hit them.

Eva

"It's about time yo ass woke up." Deray said and pecked my lips. I didn't expect to see him after finding out he slept with the ex. The last thing I remember is us arguing and him telling me something wasn't right.

"I didn't know vampires or should I say Faepyre's had morning breath." I rolled my eyes and asked where my kids and parents were.

"Your parents left this morning to get your bad ass kids from Niles who complained about them."

"My kids are not bad." He helped me sit up and then walked me in the bathroom to handle my business. When I came out he was sitting on the bed.

"Why are you here? I didn't forget what you did." I walked over to my dresser and put on a pair of sweats and a tank top. He came behind me and stood there.

"I know you didn't." He took one of my hands and intertwined it with his.

"Eva, I should've been stronger against my ex and I fucked up."

"You sure did." I turned, pushed him off and sat back on the bed.

"Whatever." He got on my nerves when he disregarded things I said.

"Anyway, I did ask your grandparents how it happened because once we imprint that's supposed to be it."

"Not that I'm accepting you back but what did they say?" I lifted my leg and put my sock on. I couldn't stand for my feet to be cold if I'm in bed.

"First off, yo ass ain't going nowhere." He pulled me in for a kiss.

"And second... someone placed a cloak over me so when we imprinted, the true love part was blocked."

"Only an elder can do that."

"It's what they said but I don't know anyone old but my grandparents. I mean they're elders but why would they block my blessing?" I put my head down blushing.

"I'm a blessing?" He lifted my head to look at him.

"They say if you find your true love it's a blessing and make sure you don't mess up." He scooted closer on the bed.

"Eva if it hadn't been for this cloak it would've never happened." We started kissing again when the door opened.

"Let me find out y'all in love already." Cal and Niles stepped in.

"Nah, it's gonna take time for that but neither one of us is going anywhere." I sucked my teeth.

"Stop doing that shit."

"What?"

"Sucking your got damn teeth. If I say we're gonna be together it is what it is."

"Say it ain't so." I heard a female's voice and turned around to see Josephine and Lenore, who Deray said resembled the fuck outta me. My brother and Niles came in shortly after.

"Hey sis." Josephine got in bed and laid her head on my shoulder.

"Say what ain't so?"

"A man got control of you."

"He ain't controlling shit."

106

"Yo, why you talking like I won't throw everyone out and fuck some common sense in you?"

"You make me sick." My other siblings walked in and Deray stared at me.

"Damn! How many of y'all are there?"

"Nine."

"NINE? Damn y'all parents were getting it in."

"You have kids?"

"Josie don't be questioning him." Cal yelled.

"Almost."

"Almost?" I asked. Those days we spent together, we spoke about a lot but he never mentioned kids.

"Yea, before I was turned my woman at the time, told me she was pregnant. We were excited as hell because the doctor said she was having twins." I could see how happy he was talking about it.

"Tragically, the night she went to deliver them, happened to be the same night I was changed."

"Wait! She knew you were a vampire?"

"We talked about it because my parents told me if I planned on marrying her she should know. She was supposed to go with me but the elders said to keep her home in case something went wrong."

"What would go wrong?"

"I don't think they wanted her to worry. The change isn't a pretty sight."

"True."

"Unbeknownst to me, she drove herself to the hospital instead of calling an ambulance. I found out later that she must've gone into labor on the way, lost control of the car and drove off a cliff."

"Oh my God." I covered my mouth.

"I'm so sorry for asking." Josephine had a sad look on her face.

"The crazy part is no one wanted to tell me once I turned. When I did find out, I lost it and had to be locked down for three months."

"Deray you don't have to talk about it."

"I'm good now but back then you couldn't tell me shit. They tried getting me to speak with psychiatrists, family members and anyone else they assumed could help." I grabbed his hand.

"It took me a year to get over that and to this day, I regret choosing this life. If I stayed home I could've driven her and she'd still be here."

"Can y'all excuse us?" I asked and heard the door close.

"Are you ok?"

"I'm good ma." I wiped the tear that fell down his face.

"Whenever I think about it, I get upset but I promise I'm good."

"Do you want kids?"

"I did but my ex ain't mother material and you and I can't have kids together." He shrugged his shoulders.

"Vampires and other vampires can't reproduce, but vampires and Faepyre's can."

"How?"

"Because were mixed with fairy, our reproductive system stayed intact. The only thing is you can only deliver once and the woman's body shuts down."

"What you mean shuts down?"

"Basically, my insides will give its own self a hysterectomy."

"Oh."

"I'm not saying we're gonna have a kid or anything but it is possible."

"If it's meant for us to have one, we will."

"Deray, you do know you can find a human to have kids with too."

"If it's not with you, I don't want any."

"I don't want you to regret not having kids."

"Shit, I haven't had any this long so I'm good." I moved over for him to join me on the bed.

"It's weird how close we've become after only knowing one another for a such a short time." I laid my head on his chest and he wrapped his arm around me.

"It is but we were placed together for a reason."

"I guess but you messed up already."

"I'm my defense, the cloak interfered with me being faithful."

"You get this one pass but if it happens again, I'm gonna make you suffer and not in a good way."

"Whatever."

"Don't underestimate my skills."

"And don't underestimate mine." He hurried to lock the door, took me in the bathroom and made love to me in there and back in the room. I wonder if he's tryna get me pregnant now because he damn sure didn't want me swallowing when I went down. I had to get up and let him cum inside me.

****

"Sooooo."

"So what?" I asked Lenore who sat across from me with Josephine.

"Hell no heffa. You about to tell us who this Deray guy is." Lenore butted in.

"Y'all met him."

"Yea but the two of you been locked up in the house for weeks now fucking each other's brains out. No one has seen you and let's not talk about the fact you're glowing." I smiled listening to my sisters saying how happy I looked.

"Glowing because I'm happy."

"All I wanna know is how is he in bed?"

"Josie, he's obviously good if they locked in the room."

"Not necessarily. Her and Faine used to be the same in the beginning."

"Yea but she was forced to change him. I don't think they ever imprinted like the rest of us; therefore, you know the sex wasn't shit."

"LENORE!"

"What? I'm just saying, if they did neither of them would be able to stop fucking."

"Faine definitely couldn't stop." Josie rolled her eyes.

"You think I wasn't good enough in bed for him?"

They looked at each other and busted out laughing.

"Girl bye. Our family are no slouches in the bedroom. It's possible that you guys just weren't a match." Lenore said, picked up the remote control and flipped the TV on.

"Shit we know Deray working with something because these bitches out here love his ass." I raised my eye at Josie.

"You may not have known who he is but his name definitely rings bells on these vampire streets."

"Really?" I was shocked because I had no clue who he was before the club incident.

"Yup. You kept your head in the books and at libraries that's why you don't know. But our husbands are well aware of who he is."

"Cal and Niles didn't know him."

"They did sis but since we weren't really worried about the war at the time, they didn't look him up."

"Oh."

"None of these bitches could get him hooked so don't underestimate your bedroom skills because he's probably not the kind who'll stick around if you suck in bed. I'm just saying." I loved my sisters because they gave it to me raw with no chaser.

They stayed at the house with me while I got ready to join Deray at the club. Now that he and I are a couple, the men in our family were always at his club. My sisters were gonna go but both of them changed their mind at the last minute. They're like me and would rather be home in the bed, then out in the club. The only reason I'm going is because my man is there. I smiled calling him that.

What's even more crazy is I already fell in love with him. I don't know if it's because he don't take my shit and fucks the hell outta me or what. All I know is I'm not letting him go and he feels the same about me.

Deray

"Tha fuck you want?" I asked my ex who came to the club and bombarded her way up the steps. I never told security she wasn't allowed here so they let her pas. After tonight, she'll never get inside this bitch again.

"Deray, you haven't been taken my calls and I hear you've been fucking that bitch Eva." I stared at her for a minute and then walked over to where she stood staring out the office window. I ran my hand up the back of her hair and snatched her head back.

"Don't talk about my woman again."

"Your woman?"

"Damn right my woman. Now again, what the fuck you want?" I pushed her away from me and she fell on the ground.

"You're getting mad at me and she's still sleeping with her kids' father."

"You're mistaken because my dick is in her every morning and night." I didn't even know why I felt the need to defend Eva sleeping with her ex when I know for a fact she's not but then again, do I? She has a lot more powers than me and can cover a lotta shit.

"That's what you think." I got a notification to my phone at the exact time she said it from an unknown number. I opened it and there was my girl Eva and some nigga. I looked up at my ex and she had a grin on her face which let me know this is a set up.

"Ok. And this means what?"

"Keep watching." She said and played with the fake dirt under her nails. You could see Eva arguing with the guy and all of sudden he had her shirt off and was sucking on her chest.

"How much more you want me to watch? Is he gonna fuck her in the video; otherwise I got shit to do." I wasn't gonna let her know how bad it hurt to see Eva in this light. I doubt she knew about him recording her but then again, I don't know with her.

"You can continue but you may get angry." It was only thirty seconds left so I entertained it. The guy went to remove her pants, winked in the camera and shut it off.

"All done. Now get the fuck out." I tossed the phone on my desk.

"Deray, you and her don't belong together."

"Oh, and a bitch who almost gave me HIV is where I belong?" I wasn't gonna bring it up because I didn't have it. I also couldn't tell her why I don't have it.

"What are you talking about?" She looked like a deer caught in headlights.

"You know exactly what I'm talking about." I showed her the screenshot of her medical records.

I went to the hospital after Eva got better and used mind compulsion on the bitch in the record area. I had her pull up my ex's file and sure shit she had the disease. She even signed off knowing about it because she had to get the medicine for it.

I may not have contracted HIV but it definitely could've killed me if I continued fucking her. That type of blood is deadly when used too much. It's the reason the bars didn't sell it but we got bootleggers too and they were selling it on the black market.

"Deray, you must've given it to me because you're the only one I slept with unprotected."

"We both know that's not true but say it is. When were you gonna tell me because you've known for almost a year now?"

"I'm not about to stand here and listen to you accuse me of being a ho because you were." I laughed at her stupid ass. She grabbed her things and headed for the door.

"Yo!" She turned around.

"If you come around me again, I'll fucking kill you." I waved her off and sent a message asking Eva where she was. When she said on the way, I prepared myself for the answer to this bullshit. If she fucking someone else we're definitely gonna have a problem. I don't give a fuck how many powers she has, I'm not about to let her play me.

I sat in my office with my hands folded like I was praying thinking about what I'm gonna say to her. I don't wanna come right out accusing her but the video is proof she's been with dude. I know its recent because when he lifted her shirt, the scar from the shooting is there.

The door opened and in she walked looking a damn runway model. She smelled different and I thought it was from her beauty products but it was something else. I wonder if it's from fucking someone else. Whatever the case we're about to find out.

"Mmmmm, I love kissing you." She backed away and her face turned up.

"She was here again."

"She was but nothing happened."

"I know because I'd be able to tell, but why was she here this time and you need a spray to remove her smell. She stinks." I chuckled and sat on the edge of my desk.

"Who the nigga you fucked or almost fucked?" She froze. I walked behind her.

"You may have a lotta powers but I promise you, I do too and will use them on your ass if you fucked him." She swung her body around fast.

"Deray, I didn't cheat on you per say." I put my arm around her neck real quick and her brother and cousin rushed through the door.

119

"Put her down or you won't live another fucking second." I felt my wrist burning by that damn light and dropped her. I guess Cal would have similar powers.

"Get the fuck out." I moved towards my desk and started healing myself with the blood I collected from my grandfather.

I went to talk to him yesterday about the cloak shit and he told me to be careful around these Faepyre's because their powers are nothing like we're used to. He started telling me about their background and how to heal myself if I were burned with the light. I'm glad he did because the shit was definitely hurting and that says a lot being I'm a vampire.

"I don't care what happened nigga, don't put your hands on my cousin." Niles was standing over top of me. I flicked my hand and he flew into the wall, only there was a wooden steak pointing at his chest.

"DERAY! Take that shit off him right now. This is between me and you." I could see Niles was mad as hell and Cal too.

"Eva, I think you and your people need to go."

120

"Take that shit off him." She pointed to the steak and tapped her feet waiting. I sucked my teeth and did it. Regardless of how mad I was, she definitely had my heart and could get me to do whatever for her. I hadn't told her yet, but a nigga is definitely in love.

"NIGGA!" Eva intercepted the two of us from getting ready to fight by using her light to put a clear glass or something up. Every day she surprised me with her powers.

"ENOUGH!" She shouted because we were going back and forth.

"Cal and Niles, I love y'all for protecting me but let me handle this."

"Fuck that Eva. He doing dumb shit and…"

"I got it y'all. He won't hurt me, will you?" She looked at me and I waved my hand at her. She knew me like a fucking book and I hated it.

"Give us a minute." Neither one of them wanted to leave but did on the strength of her. When the door closed she ran up and pushed me against the wall.

"Don't ever in your fucking life put your hands on me again."

"Hold up."

"NO, YOU HOLD THE FUCK UP!" She backed away.

"I was coming to tell you about the situation and had you given me time, I would've. Instead, you get in your feelings and I get it but what you're not gonna do is take out the frustrations you have with your ex on me." I tried to speak but she wouldn't let me.

"I smelled her the second the door opened but I didn't accuse you of anything." I pushed her out the way and went to my desk.

"I don't give a fuck what you're saying right now Eva because the situations are different."

"How?"

"Because you let the nigga take your clothes off and suck on your fucking titties. You were kissing him like he was me. That's some ho shit and I don't care if you get mad; I said it." She went to open her mouth and I put my hand up for her to be quiet.

"And before you even think of bringing up me cheating on you, don't. We moved past that shit and found out why it happened. You on the other hand was on some sneaky shit."

"Deray?"

"I don't wanna fucking hear it. Whatever you were tryna accomplish or whatever information you wanted from him, shouldn't have required you to be naked or touching him in any way." She put her head down because she knew I was right.

"Then you waltz up in here like, *I didn't cheat on you per say*. Like the shit is a fucking joke, so hell yea I was about to choke you the fuck out." I slammed my hand on the desk.

"YOU'RE MY FUCKING WOMAN EVA AND YOU DISRESPECTED THE SHIT OUTTA ME AND OUR RELATIONSHIP. THA FUCK WERE YOU THINKING?" She had me on fire right now.

"Uhmmm, ok." She picked her things up and headed to the door.

"I'll make sure Niles and Cal don't address you about this again."

"I don't give a fuck about that because it's what they're supposed to do. You're their family so I expected it, but you can let them know they pump no fear here. If they wanna get it popping, we can." She made her way to the door and turned around.

"The guy in the video is my kids' father. I was trying to get him to tell me who he was working for because he's supposedly tryna come up with a plan to hurt me." I can see her going to ask questions but getting naked is where I draw the line. She went overboard and no one is gonna make me see it differently.

"Let me get this right." I stood and walked over to her.

"You heard he's working with someone to hurt you and the first thing you do is take your ass over there alone? That makes no sense." She didn't say anything.

"I wasn't thinking and I thought he'd tell me."

"You thought he'd tell you if you got naked, and in front of a got damn camera Eva?"

"I didn't know he was recording and I'm sorry you saw it but I won't apologize for doing what I needed to keep my family safe."

"There were other ways Eva and you know it." She wiped her eyes.

"You're right but I was in a rush because I didn't want anyone else to get hurt. Looks like I'm the only one who did."

"You're the only one huh?" I went back to my desk, sat down, put my feet on it and placed my hands on my stomach.

"You think watching that video didn't hurt me? You say, y'all didn't do shit but I don't know that for sure. At least when I slept with my ex you didn't see it. FUCK! Those images are never gonna leave my mind."

"Deray."

"Just go Eva. I can't even look at you right now." She nodded and I turned my head. I didn't wanna talk to her like that but I was hurt like a motherfucker at the moment.

When she closed the door, I looked up all the info on her kids' father and made plans to make a visit. He needs to see I don't play about mine.

Niles

"What happened up there?" Kat asked when we stormed out the club. We refused to leave Eva but we didn't feel like staying in the club either. Cal was able to tell us what they were saying inside the office because Eva let him in her head.

I understood why he felt the way he did and I probably would've reacted the same but that steak shit to my chest was unnecessary. Once he removed it, hell yea I was ready to fight and so was Cal. Of course, Eva wouldn't allow it to happen and I'm sure it's because they'll eventually get back together. I don't care if they do or not, that nigga gonna see me.

"Eva did some foul shit tryna get information and he must've found out."

"What?"

"Yea and he choked her so we went in there. Can you believe that motherfucker had the nerve to choke her?" Kat looked at me because I did it to her once.

"That's because you were tryna leave me."

"It doesn't make it right."

"It's different because she's my cousin."

"And I'm your wife." I could see her getting angry and tried to diffuse the situation.

"This is not about us and I don't wanna argue." We saw Eva coming towards us looking upset.

"You ok?" Kat hugged her and out the corner of my eye I saw this stupid bitch. I knew she was about to say something and tried to rush Kat to the car but it didn't work.

"Megan what are you doing here?" Kat asked and I walked away. I hated this bitch with a passion.

"We need to talk. Can I come over?"

"Nope." I said loud enough for her to hear. She was tryna find any way to get over my house.

"Niles. She's upset and crying."

"Not our problem. I'm ready to go." I hit the alarm on the car and if shit couldn't get worse, here comes one of the women I used to mess with. Kat wasn't paying us any mind and Cal was busy on the phone with some new chick he met.

"Hey sexy." My wife damn near flew in our direction. I guess she was listening.

"You keep testing me bitch. I got something for your ass."

"You sure do. All this good dick you keeping to yourself." Why did the bitch say that? Kat snatched her by the hair and drug her around the corner. Megan tried to follow but Eva stopped her.

"Get your fucking hands off me." Me, Cal and Eva gave her a look. Eva only had her hand on Megan's arm. She didn't grab her or anything like that and the bitch started tripping.

"What you say?" Eva had a look in her eye we all knew too well. She was about to make Megan disappear forever.

"You heard me. Don't put your hands on me."

"I don't know what your problem is Megan but it's best if you calm the fuck down."

"Bitch please. You think because you're fucking Deray I'm supposed to be worried?" Now I see exactly why she was

128

tripping. She must be fucking him too or used to. It's the only reason I could think of as to why she's bugging.

"What? Who told you that?"

"Everyone knows you're spreading your legs to any man out here willing to get in between." She laughed and Eva smacked fire from her. I saw Cal moving in and ran to check on my wife.

By the time I made it to her, she was finishing off the bitch who approached me. I mean there wasn't anything left of her except hair and a few bones.

I heard a noise and turned because the heartbeat was loud and beating very fast. I sniffed around and found some young kid scared as hell. I lifted her up, erased her memory and sent her on her way.

I took my shirt off and wiped Kat's face because blood was dropping outta her mouth and specks were on her face. The shit turned me on to see her devouring food and I almost pulled my dick out to fuck her. Unfortunately, I heard Cal telling me to get out there because Faine just popped up and Deray is on his way out.

"Come on."

"Niles, I have blood on me."

"You're fine." We walked over to Eva and Megan and outta nowhere, Megan smacked my cousin and chaos broke out.

Deray literally threw Megan across the parking lot and Cal had to stop Eva from turning her to ashes. Faine said some slick shit to Deray about fucking my cousin, and he beat the fuck outta him. We had to pull him off because humans were coming out recording and you could hear the cops in the distant. I could care less if he went to jail but I know my cousin would have a fit and I don't feel like hearing her mouth.

"We gotta go."

"Niles, I have to check on my sister. Deray why did you do that?" He was watching Eva erase everyone's memory and snatching up the phones outta the people's hands. We all looked at her.

"Kat you know she deserved that."

"But she's pregnant."

"You know it ain't mine." Deray said. It was like time stood still.

"Why would it be yours or would it be a possibility?" Before Deray could answer Eva, cops swarmed in and we all left. I could tell Eva was hurt but why? Even if he did sleep with Megan it was before her time. *What a fucking night?*

****

"Why would your sisters baby possibly be Deray's?" Kat and I just finished showering and was getting ready for bed.

"Niles they've been together for a couple of years."

"What?"

"Yea. He's the one who threw her out and..."

"Wait a minute. Wait a minute." I was tryna wrap my mind around this whole scenario.

"She's been with him all this time and had no idea who he was?"

"Yup."

"I'm not gonna ask how's that possible but I do wanna know how she pregnant? We know damn well it ain't his."

"I can't even tell you baby because ever since he cheated on her, she's been screwing any and every one. Do you

131

think she was sleeping with Faine?" I shrugged my shoulders and got in the bed to watch a movie.

"It's no telling with her." She snuggled up next to me.

"As long as she didn't sleep with my husband I don't care." She rested her head on my chest and we laid there watching movies all night. Megan better not ever tell my wife or I promise she's a dead bitch walking.

Eva

After hearing Kat shout out her sister's pregnancy; nothing shocked me more than Deray yelling it wasn't his. Not that I could be mad but why didn't he mention they used to be a couple? Yes, it's his business; however, he knows how cool I am with Kat and they're sisters. Whatever the reason it doesn't matter because he made it clear it's over.

I pulled up in my driveway and let my head fall back on the seat. How could I be so stupid and try to persuade Faine? I had no business letting him get as far as he did. We definitely didn't have sex though. I wasn't about to allow any man to touch me, even though the urge was there.

My grandmother wasn't lying when she said regardless of us imprinting on each other, sex with other people is still possible. I didn't even want sex with Faine but when he was kissing on me and sucking in my chest, I was ready. It took everything in me, not to go through with it.

I picked my phone up and called Deray just to see if he'd answer. In the short time I left the club, I was missing him already.

"What?" He barked and let me know he's still mad. At least he answered the phone for me.

"I'm sorry." The phone went silent.

"I should've never gone to his house or allowed him to touch me. As your woman, I had the responsibility to let you handle it."

"Eva maybe the cloak interfering with us imprinting is a sign. I mean you did something stupid and it made me fuck my ex. It could be a sign we don't belong together."

"Is that what you believe?" I heard him blow his breath.

"I want you Eva but if this is how you are all the time, I'm gonna pass. I mean my woman thought using sex was ok."

"Deray, I swear we didn't sleep together."

"It don't even matter. You should've never been there."

I wiped the tears falling from my eyes. I couldn't believe this

134

man had me so vulnerable and open. I wanted and needed him in my life and he no longer felt the same.

"I'm sorry for hurting you Deray. I wanted to tell you that."

"Are you home?"

"Yea. I'm about to go in the house."

"A'ight." Both of us stayed on the phone because neither wanted to say goodbye.

"Boss, the cops are still here." I heard a guy's voice in the background.

"Eva, I gotta go."

"Uhmmm ok. I'll talk to you later." I hung the phone up, stepped out my car and went in the house. My phone went off and I looked at the text message.

Deray: *Give me some time Eva. If it's meant for us to be together; I'll come find you.* I didn't respond. All I could do is respect his decision.

****

"Faine what are you doing here?" I opened the door and folded my arms. The kids weren't here because with us not knowing who's behind these vampire hunters, I couldn't take the chance of anything happening to them.

"My kids live here." I busted out laughing.

"Oh, now you have kids?"

"Don't be like that Eva. Move." He tried to step in but couldn't because his invitation has been rescinded for a long time now.

"Why did you send that video to Deray?" It's been a month since it happened and neither of us reached out to the other.

"Fuck him."

"Why is that?"

"I think you know why."

"Why don't you tell me?" I had no clue why he didn't like Deray.

"Eva, you know I want us together." I tossed my head back laughing. He got mad and tried moving past me again.

"Can you invite me in so I can see my kids?"

"They're not here." I went to close the door but he put his foot there to block me.

"Where the fuck are they?"

"None of your business." He snatched me by the hair and drug me out the door. I tried gripping his hand to pry him off but I couldn't. I summoned Cal in my head and he claimed he was too far to get me but he's calling my mom.

I didn't wanna call my other siblings because they're all married and so are my cousins. Deray's angry with me so he blocked me from his brain somehow. His ass had to be researching Faepyre's because he was doing a lotta shit I thought I only knew.

"Yea, ain't nobody here to help you." My legs were on the ground getting scraped up and as much as I tried protecting myself it wasn't working. I didn't want him tryna take me away so I summoned my father, grandfather and anyone else who could hear me. He must've known someone would eventually come because he dropped me by the gate, stomped me in the face and all over my body. I was going to heal with no problem but my child won't. I grabbed my stomach in front of him by accident and he flipped.

"You let that stupid motherfucker get you pregnant? I'm gonna make sure that baby doesn't survive." He went to kick me in the stomach and I used every bit of power in my body to push him away.

It wasn't far but he couldn't get back in the gate. I noticed my sisters come in and once they saw him, put an invisible wall around that no one could see but us. He tried numerous times to get in and finally gave up and left.

"I told you not to be alone Eva. This is not your normal pregnancy." My grandmother Ambrosia said flying in and asked my sisters to help her get me inside.

"Where's daddy?"

"Eva all the guys are at a conference. Did you forget?" My mom flew in like a bat outta hell and started crying.

"Where's Deray?" Lenore asked.

"Sis he doesn't know yet."

"Why not?"

"I planned on calling tonight and telling him."

I've been giving him time to cool off and stayed away. And as much as I missed him, I took responsibility for doing something stupid. I had no business allowing Faine to touch me inappropriately to get information that he didn't even give.

"Call your other grandmother over here. We need to know how to heal her." The pain was excruciating and usually blood would heal but with this baby being conceived differently, we we're still learning the side effects.

"Mommy it hurts really bad." My face was in a lotta pain. The force from his foot is ten times worse than the feeling a human would have if they did it. For some reason my body wasn't healing fast enough; therefore, I was feeling everything.

"Is the baby ok?" Ambrosia placed her hand on my stomach.

"Right now, he is. We need to get you healed because he'll go into distress soon." I nodded and tried my hardest not to stress but it's hard.

Deray and I discussed having a baby together and he went right out to get the serum that unfreezes his sperm. I swear we were going at it every day. That's why my family said we were locked in the house for so long. We were making sure I got pregnant.

I found out the night Faine sent him the video and went to the club to tell him. Unfortunately, things went left so I never mentioned it. I could've still told him but I wanted us to be cordial first. I didn't want him to think I only told him to stay together. Now that I think of it, I should've because this wouldn't have happened.

"He?"

"I'm sorry honey it slipped out."

"It's ok. I'm sure he'll be happy to know there will be an heir for him in general."

"Eva I'm going to give you some of my blood." My mom and sisters looked at her.

Ambrosia is supposedly the Lilith which is the most powerful vampire out there. I mean she's more powerful than my grandfather in ways. If she gives me her blood, they're not sure if it will affect who I am because of all the different things we're both mixed with.

"We don't have a choice. She's dying." All of them stared at me and my mother told her to hurry up and do it.

"Fuck this. What's his address?" Josie said and I told her to check the club first. Soon as she left, my body began shutting down more.

Faine

"How are you?" I asked Megan when I stepped in her hospital room. Both of us got in some shit at the club but I was able to heal myself and she wasn't. Her ass been in this hospital ever since.

I thought about checking on her sooner but wasn't sure if Deray had people watching her. I didn't need him coming for me again and I was unprepared. Next time, I had something for his ass though. It didn't mean I wasn't gonna take my anger out on Eva though.

Word on the street is her and Deray are no longer together, which is exactly why I went over there. Unfortunately, when I saw her clutch her stomach I knew she was expecting and lost it. She isn't supposed to give another man a baby. What the fuck was she thinking? I tried to kill the bitch and would've if her sisters didn't show up.

Once I was out the gate, I couldn't get back in but I was able to get her with the syringe. It pissed me off I couldn't watch her die. You damn right I was on some, *if I couldn't have her, no one will.*

"Fine!" She looked down at her leg that was held up in the air by some rope. Both of her arms were broken, and so was her nose.

"You don't look fine." I moved closer to her.

"What do you want Faine?" I sat in the chair grinning.

"First off, don't get upset with me because you stuck up here. How you end up in here anyway?" I saw what happened at the club but unsure of what transpired first.

"Your fucking ex." She rolled her eyes.

"Eva did this?"

"No, my ex did."

"Huh?" She began explaining how her and Deray had it out in his office. She went outside and got into an argument with Eva. Things went left from that point on.

"You know I can heal you." Her eyes grew wide.

"How so?"

"Duh. I'm a vampire." I whispered.

"If you drink my blood, it'll heal you instantly."

"Really?"

"Yup but I'll only do it if you do something for me." I walked over to close the door when in walked two women. One I knew off the bat was like me. She was Niles wife and they've been together for a while too. I stared at her and Megan and blinked my eyes a few times. The two of them were damn near identical, besides the hair color and mole.

"Why are you here?" Megan asked as her twin stood on the side of her.

"I came to see if you're ok."

"It's been a month Kat and you just coming up here?"

"Megan, I have kids to take care of and mommy kept me updated."

"I'm fine. You can go." I don't know why she's snapping on her. I'd be happy if any of my family members showed up after suffering an accident such as hers. Some people are so ungrateful.

"I don't know what your problem is with me lately but I suggest you tone it the fuck down."

"Ok ladies. You're sisters."

144

"Ma, anybody who's friends with a woman I'm not, isn't my sister."

"Megan you and Eva not being friends or even cordial is your fault."

"How so?"

"You were always getting smart with her, and you smacked her at the club. Why would you even assume she'd be ok with that?"

"Fuck her and you. Both of you bitches can kiss my ass."

"Bitch? Was I a bitch when I gave you money to stay in a hotel even when my husband said no? Was I a bitch when I got your ass a car in my name? Was I a bitch when my husband...?"

"Your husband?" Megan tossed her head back laughing but you could see she was in pain.

"The same husband who cheated on you with tons of bitches?"

"Megan don't start your shit." Her mom tried to diffuse the situation but it wasn't working.

145

"You've never been happy for me Megan. It's always been competition with you and I don't know why."

"Ain't no competition sis."

"Yes it is. You're mad I got a house, husband and..."

"Bitch stop praising your husband because he ain't shit."

"That's why you don't have a man because you're so hateful." She laughed again. Her sister was on her way out and stopped.

"I don't need a man when I have yours to fuck." It's like the entire room got quiet. Megan's mom covered her mouth in shock and her sister didn't know what to say at first. I could see her staring and thinking of what to say next.

"I know for a fact you're not fucking my husband."

"Do you?" Megan smirked.

"Let me fill you in on your perfect husband."

"Megan stop this shit right now." Her mother tried to intervene again but it wasn't working. I was curious myself because that nigga Niles be on some crazy shit over his wife. I know he didn't fuck her sister. But then again, they look exactly alike.

"The night you were supposed to go home after he cheated and you left, I went by the house thinking you were there. He was in the shower so I stayed downstairs fixing myself something to eat."

"How did you get in?"

"Duh, you gave me the key for emergencies." Her sister shook her head.

"Anyway, you were always bragging about how good he was in bed and how big it is, so I decided to try him out. I have to admit sis, he is pretty big and I sucked his soul out. Mmmmm, I still remember how his cum tasted."

"You're lying." I could see Kat getting angrier and knew shit was about to go left.

"It sucks to be identical, doesn't it? He definitely enjoyed it."

"I don't believe you."

"Ask him. You know he's never been a good liar so you'll know." She smirked.

"I mean he swore I was you or maybe he knew it wasn't you. They say men love fucking twins." All I know is her sister lost it.

She picked her ass up out the bed and threw her across the room. When her body hit the ground, she started banging her head over and over. Blood was gushing out. If I didn't stop Kat, she was gonna kill her.

"Kat stop it." Her mom cried out and she pushed her back.

"Did you know?" She asked her mother who was petrified. I would be too because Kat's eyes were now red and her fangs were visible.

"I thought she was lying."

"You two better not ever come around me again. Do I make myself clear?"

"Kat you're one of them too?" She let her fangs go back in and her eyes returned to normal.

"Yup and if you or her even think about opening your mouth, I promise to return and eat both of you myself." And just like that, she disappeared.

I helped her mom try and lift Megan but it was no use. She was almost dead and I could hear her heartbeat slowing down. Her mom asked if I knew any vampires who could heal her.

I stood, closed the door, let my fangs down and tore into my flesh. I told her she needed to make sure her daughter agreed to help. Once she did, I let Megan feed off me and regretted it.

"Bitch you had HIV?"

"Had?" She questioned slowly healing and then getting off the ground.

"My blood healed you but I tasted it in your blood stream when you kissed me. You lucky as hell I wore condoms with your trifling ass." I don't know why I didn't notice it before.

"She doesn't have it anymore?" Her mother seemed to be pleased.

"No."

"Oh my God, thank you." She hugged me.

"Now what?"

"Now we get outta here and finish off the plan."

"And what's that?" I put her in my arms.

"We're about to get rid of Eva, her family, Deray and anyone else who gets in the way."

"Why are you doing this?"

"Save those questions for another day. We gotta get the fuck outta here." I scooped her up and exited the hospital as fast as I could. It's no telling when they'll come looking for us after Kat tells her husband what happened. Shit, I'm surprised they haven't found me yet after finding Eva, but then again, the cloak has hidden me well.

Deray

"How much longer you gonna be mad at her?" My mother asked and took a seat next to me on the couch. I stopped by to see her and my grandfather who's been staying here. My parents had a huge house too and my mother wanted her mom and dad here until this war crap is over.

"I don't even know." I was missing the fuck outta Eva.

"Explain to me what happened again." I sat there telling her as I stared at the ceiling.

"Ok. Now I'm playing devil's advocate here son." I sucked my teeth because I know she was about to take Eva's side.

"You slept with your ex because the cloak interfered right?"

"Yea."

"And she forgave you right?"

"Yea but it's different." She smiled.

"Deray you're stubborn like your father and when people piss you off, you shut down or cut them off." I remained silent.

"I understand what she did was stupid regardless if it were for a good reason in her eyes or not. And I also understand how you feel seeing the video, but how do you think she felt knowing you made love you to your ex, the way you did her?"

"What?"

"She may not have witnessed a video but she knows how you make her feel in the bedroom and knows you did the same for your ex."

"Nah. Eva has given me the best sex ever and I'd never make love to her the same way." She put her hand up.

"It doesn't matter. You still slept with another woman whether it was accidental or not." I ran my hand over my head.

"Son if you love her, I suggest you get over this and be with her. Otherwise; every day the two of you don't speak will make her think it's over. Then what? You're gonna be mad if she finds someone else."

152

"She ain't never gonna be with anyone else."

"Well that's selfish." I shrugged my shoulders.

"Call her son." She kissed my cheek and went in the kitchen to give me and my grandfather private time.

He's one of the elders who helps turn humans into vampires. He's been around for a very long and told me I should research all I can on fairies because if I planned on being with Eva, I should know everything there is.

"What you want nigga? I'm about to watch some vampire porn." I almost fell off the couch from laughing so hard.

"How do we get this cloak thing fixed? I'm not about to let Eva fuck no one else."

"Why not? You don't want her."

"Gramps, I do want her. I just wanna make sure she don't do anymore dumb shit."

"Listen nephew."

"Nephew? You're my grandfather."

"I know but it sounds better saying nephew." I shook my head because my grandfather is a trip.

"What she did is wrong; I agree. But if she went over there to get the information it must be something else going on."

"What you mean?"

"Eva has powers none of us have ever seen before. She can get a person to do and say things they don't want. Its obvious this Faine dude has some sort of cover over him, otherwise she could get into his mind." I listened to my gramps talk and it did make sense but she still should've let me handle it, or at least go with her.

"Me and her grandfather Ambrogio have been talking and we believe Faine is going to try and kill her for not wanting him."

"WHAT?" I hopped out my seat.

"Don't worry, he's nowhere near as powerful as her." He gave me a look that said whatever he's about to say is gonna piss me off.

"Whoever he's working with is giving him vital information, in which, she may already be in harm's way."

"But how?"

"He has to come around for the kids. All she has to do is let him in and that's it. He'll be able to attack."

"FUCK!" I stood and grabbed my things to leave.

"Bring Eva to her grandparents' house because no one can reach her there no matter what kind of spell they have."

"Why haven't the guys taken her there?"

"I literally just hung up with Ambrogio right before you got here. They're all at a meeting and he wanted me to ask you to get her."

"A'ight. Let me finish what I have to do at the club and I'll go."

"Hurry up Deray because it's no telling what the Faine dude has up his sleeve."

"Ok. I'll let you know when I get there." I flew outta there and rushed to the club so I can get her. I still have her ass in time out but I'm not about to let anything happen to her either.

****

"When the group performs, make sure the sound system is exactly the way they want." I told the crew in my club.

Some guy rented the entire club out for a private party and I wanted it to be perfect. That way he'll post it on social media and bring in more business. Yes, we do everything humans do if you haven't figured it out.

"Boss, some lady here to see you." I heard the manager say over the intercom.

"Take her name and number and tell her I'll call later. I'm busy." I was rushing to do everything so I could bounce.

"Uhmmm, this one isn't taking no for an answer." I turned the camera on in my office and blew my breath out.

"Send her up." I prepared myself for this bullshit, knowing damn well I didn't wanna hear it. I met her at the door.

"What did you do to my daughter?" Megan's mom shouted and pushed past me.

When I saw Megan put her hands on Eva, I lost it and tossed the bitch across the parking lot. She fell on top of a car

156

and smashed the windshield. Her face was bleeding and she had a few broken bones for sure. Megan of all people knows I don't play that bullshit.

"She tried to come for my woman at the time and got what she deserved. You of all people know I don't play about my woman." She sucked her teeth but she knew.

I cursed her out quite a few times over the way she used to speak to Megan. When we lived together she tried telling me what to do in my own house. Mother or not, I let her know she wasn't running shit in my crib.

"Your woman? When did you and my daughter break up?"

"We've been broken up for a while now. Did you know she had HIV?"

"I told her to tell you."

"You knew too?" I gave her a hard stare.

"She don't even know where she got it from. I thought it was you but then I heard about who you were and knew it wasn't. Why didn't you heal her with your blood?"

"What the fuck you say?"

"Ughhh."

"Don't ugh now. What did you just say?" I hemmed her up.

"Megan said someone told her about vampires and you were one. Please don't kill me."

"When did she tell you?" If Megan told her mom it's no telling who else she told.

"A while ago."

"Where is the bitch now?"

"I don't know. Some guy came to the hospital, gave her some of his blood and left with her."

"What did he look like?" She started describing some guy who sounded like Eva's ex but until I saw him, I couldn't be sure. Once she told me about Kat beating Megan up for sleeping with her husband, I knew shit was about to be hectic.

"Get out." I grabbed my keys, walked to the door and ran into one of Eva's sisters.

"Who the fuck are you?" This bitch didn't know when to shut the fuck up. Josie looked her up and down.

"BAM!" She slammed Megan's mom face into the door and her body hit the ground. I think her nose was broken.

"Where have you been? Eva's been tryna contact you."

"We've been taking a break. I'm sure she told you."

"Look Deray, I don't care what type of attitude you have with my sister. I need you to come with me."

"For?" I folded my arms. I was on my way to go get her, but I wanted to know what she was talking about.

"Faine beat her up real bad and she's dying."

"WHAT?" I looked to see if she were serious. Once that tear fell, I flew outta there and straight to Eva's house. We may not be speaking but to hear she's dying is doing something to me.

"Where is she?" Lenore had the door opened before I made it to the front.

"Deray before you go in there be prepared."

"Prepared for what?" I didn't wait to hear her response and rushed to the room. I was at a loss for words by the way she looked. Her eyes were barely open and swollen; her skin was pale and bruises were all over her body.

159

"When did this happen?"

"A few hours ago."

"And y'all just now came to get me?" I was aggravated as fuck with them.

"We thought she'd heal on her own."

"Why does she look like this? Her body should be healing itself." They all stared at me.

"He doesn't know." I rubbed Eva's hair as she whispered something I wanted to hear but didn't expect.

"I'm pregnant Deray." I smiled hard as hell. We were trying and I had no idea we succeeded.

"Do you need my blood to heal? What's going on?"

"Deray when she mentioned having a baby she kept a few things from you."

"Ok what?"

"Each day she's pregnant, her strength dwindles. Therefore; her powers weaken as well." I stared down at her.

"She's nowhere near as strong as she usually is and anyone can attack and it'll be nothing she can do."

"Why didn't you tell me?"

"I wanted to give you a baby Deray."

"But it's killing you. Take it out." I glanced over at Ambrosia. I knew all about her being the Lilith and knew she could do the procedure just by touching her.

"She's only two months and the baby won't survive."

"I don't care. If it's killing her, take it out."

"NO!!!" She shouted as loud as she could.

"There's a way to keep the baby and get my strength back."

"What?"

"Faine has to die."

"He's gonna die anyway for doing this to you." She grabbed my hand.

"Deray, he stabbed me with a syringe and in it was the same stuff I got shot with before." I gave her a crazy look. Humans did that shit so how was he responsible for doing it to her?

"He's working with an elder and the vampire hunters."

"You gotta be fucking kidding me." I was fuming.

"Where the fuck is he?" I jumped up and waited for her to answer.

"Deray he's my kids father and..."

"You have a choice to make Eva. Either you want me to kill him or I want this baby outta you, right fucking now. There's no way in hell I'm risking your life for a nigga."

"But the baby.-"

"Of course I want the baby but not like this Eva. It's killing you." I felt tears rolling down my face. I knew then. I would be no good if I lost another woman I loved.

"I love you Deray." I sat next to her.

"I love you too ma." I pecked her lips and watched as she grimaced in pain just by me touching her. I hated what this nigga did and he needed to be dealt with ASAP.

"Eva tell me where he is." Her eyes started fluttering and her body jerked. Everyone started panicking and so did I.

"EVA! EVAAAAAA!"

To Be Continued....